Merry Mischief List

HAILEY DICKERT

Copyright © 2023 by Hailey Rose Dickert

First released December 2023.

ISBN: 978-1-960497-05-5

Developmental Editing: Alli Morgan

Copy Editing: Anonymous

Proofreading: Caitlin Lengerich

Cover: Maldo Designs

Published by Hailey Dickert

www.haileydickert.com

CRYSTAL BAY UNIVERSITY

BOOK TWO

Author's Note

Merry Mischief List is the second installment in Hailey Dickert's Crystal Bay University Series. While the main characters in this story are initially introduced in the first novel, **Return Policy**, **Merry Mischief List** can be read as a standalone.

There are multiple sexually explicit scenes in this novel. Whether you want to be naughty or nice, there's a Dicktionary to find (or avoid) the smut quickly, which can be found on page 176.

This book contains topics that could be uncomfortable for some readers. For a complete list, please see the Content Warnings on page 177.

Playlist

'The Last Twerk Before Christmas' Playlist

Reindeer (Pony - Christmas version) — Furnace and the Fundamentals
Christmas Lap Dance (Radio Edit) — R-Dot
Deck The Halls (Trap Remix) — Bass Boosted HD, DJ Remix, Christmas Songs Remix
A Nonsense Christmas — Sabrina Carpenter
Fa La La — Justin Bieber, Boyz II Men
Naughty List (with Dixie) — Liam Payne, Dixie
buy me presents — Sabrina Carpenter
Like It's Christmas — Jonas Brothers
Wrap Me Up — Jimmy Fallon, Meghan Trainer
is it new years yet? — Sabrina Carpenter
I Saw Mommy Kissing Santa Claus — The Jackson 5

Sorry, Mom. Sex sells.
Especially when it's wrapped with a holiday bow.

1
ANDI

"I'm swearing off women. And men. And non-binary people. And anyone else who could possibly screw me over." I huff, staring up at the ceiling from my position on the couch.

"So what's that leave you with? Aliens? Vivian the vibrator?" Stella, my apparently heartless roommate, asks.

"Hey, vibrators are a girl's best friend," I argue.

"What happened to diamonds?"

"Diamonds never gave me an orgasm."

"True..." she agrees, narrowing her eyes. "But why are you acting all butt hurt? *You* dumped *her.*"

"I mean... I wouldn't say I *dumped* her, per se."

"I believe your exact words were 'Fuck you and your judgy high horse, Olivia. Go find some boring bitch who wants to mope in the corner of every bar if that's what you really want,'" she says, as if I need a reminder of the fight I've been thinking about all week.

"That is a *horrible* misquote. I believe my *actual* exact

words were 'If you want some shy girl who hides in the corner of every bar, that's never gonna be me.'"

"And?" Stella rolls her hand for me to continue, and I blow out a raspberry in defeat.

"'And if that's what you really want, you should go to Boring Bitch 'R' Us to find someone new to screw.'"

"Like I said." Stella laughs, shaking her head.

"Oh my god, you're right." I groan. "I *dumped* her two weeks before Christmas! Who even does that?"

"Someone who was sick of being caged like a prized show tiger?"

"What if I'm looking at this all wrong?" I ask, grabbing the open bottle of wine from our coffee table and taking a swig. "What if *I'm* the villain here? Me!"

"Seriously, cut this shit out." Stella hops off the loveseat she was perched on and comes over, snatching the wine bottle. "Olivia was an asshole. All she ever tried to do was change you."

Why does Stella always have to be right? As much as I enjoyed spending time with Olivia, she did consistently pressure me to tone down the person I am. I was always "too" something. Too loud. Too crazy. Too happy. Too friendly. Too energetic. Whatever it was, it was *too much* for her.

"You are *not* the monster in this story, babe," Stella continues, moving my legs to take a seat next to me on the couch. "Please don't let this one judgmental sorority girl keep you from all humankind."

"*Maybe* I'll consider giving the human race a second chance before jumping on the faerie smut bandwagon," I reply.

"Good. So are you done with this pity fest? Ready to be the Grinch-ess who stole back Christmas?"

"Are you seriously calling me the Grinch? Aren't you supposed to be supporting me right now?"

"Girl, have you seen the movie? The Grinch ends up being the freaking *hero*! He saves Christmas, *and* his heart grows three sizes. So yes, you're the Grinch right now, but Christmas shall be saved!" she shouts, throwing her arms in the air with full-on jazz hands.

"Okay, Dr. Seuss. A bit theatrical, don't you think?" I say, laughing at her antics.

"No, I think it's the perfect amount of enthusiasm for the situation at hand," she replies, pinning me with a single look.

"Well, how do you suggest I steal back Christmas? I don't know of a holiday Whobilation happening anytime soon."

"Hmm," Stella hums mindlessly, pulling out her phone.

"*Helllooo?*" I ask. "Currently in the middle of a crisis here. What are you doing?"

"Searching 'how not to have a shitty Christmas.'"

"I don't think Google can solve this issue."

"Hah! Wrong again, Andi-kins," she says, hopping off the couch. "I've found the perfect idea." She runs out of the room and comes back with a piece of paper and a pen.

"Are we asking Santa to add Olivia to the naughty list?"

"Funny, but no," she quips. "We're making you a merry to-do list."

"A what?"

"A to-do list. Like, 'I'm gonna do all this fun-ass shit to stop being miserable for Christmas.' We're both going to winter wonderlands with full on Christmas vibes. We gotta capitalize on that stuff."

"I'm pretty sure *I'm* the only one getting the *true* Christmas vibes," I point out. "You're going to party at a ritzy ski lodge with Theo while I sing Christmas carols with Aunt Delilah."

"Oh, come on. You know you're gonna need a distraction from this Olivia shit and the Jess Show."

"That's true..." I internally groan at the thought of my older sister. Anytime we try to have a conversation, she always flips it back on herself and how great her life is.

It's exhausting.

Stella taps the pen against the paper impatiently. "So can we make this list or what?"

"Fine," I agree. "What will we be adding to said merry dumpmas list?"

"Yes! Hmm, okay... Build a snowman?"

"That's something I can get on board with."

She scribbles it down and adds five more items to the list:

Ice skating

Snowball fight

Kiss under mistletoe

Drink spiked hot chocolate

Decorate a Christmas tree

"I see you're taking a page out of every Hallmark Christmas movie ever made. Very original," I tease.

"Well, I figure it's hard to paint yourself the villain when you're doing all this merry shit. But if you want *original*, let's be original." She boops my nose with a pen, a mischievous smile spreading across her face. "Let's add... gingerbread man tower."

I choke on a laugh. "What does that even mean?"

"You know… an Eiffel Tower? A threesome? A ménage à trois?"

"Okay, okay." I wave her off. "I get it."

"Oh!" she exclaims, crossing out the gingerbread man tower. "That's not very inclusive. What if you find a hot Mrs. Claus to join?"

"Good idea. There's a girl I hooked up with last year I wouldn't mind a round two with." *And three. And four.*

"What about… triple gumdrop tower? It's gender neutral."

"Perfect. And add 'bake gingerbread cookies,'" I suggest, thinking of one of my favorite traditions.

"Really? Use your imagination! Don't be so basic."

"But the art of cookie baking is *very* merry."

"How about…" She scribbles down, *Bake gingerbread man cookies (XLGD).*

"XLGD?"

"Yeah, extra-large ginger dick."

"You want me to bake gingerbread men with giant dicks?" I scoff. "My grandma makes the dough!"

"Sorry." She shrugs. "It's on the list. I don't make the rules."

"You're literally the one making the rules." I roll my eyes in mock annoyance. "You know what? If you're making me do this ridiculous shit, you're doing it too."

I snatch the pen from her and scribble *Merry Mischief List* at the top.

"Oh, okay, that's cute," she says. "What are the stakes?"

I glance down at the list, feeling confident she'll avoid a few of these. "Loser has to streak outside our hotel after the bowl game in Arizona on New Year's Eve."

"Deal." She snatches the paper back. "But we're not done with the list." Excitement floods my veins at the idea of a challenge. "You have to block Olivia."

And my stomach drops to my feet. "Oh, come on. That'll cause drama. It's so unnecessary." *It's actually probably a hundred percent necessary.* Olivia's been sending messages since the day of our "breakup" and I expected them to stop, but they just keep on coming.

OLIVIA

I can't believe you said all that in front of everyone

Then again you are a cheerleader, so I should know by now you like an audience

Everything always has to be about YOU. Was it really so bad I didn't want you twerking like a fucking whore on the middle of the dance floor?

Sorry. That last one was a little harsh. It was more like a hooker

Seriously the silent treatment?

Grow up and talk to me like an adult.

"Well, *not* blocking her is gonna cause drama in your heart, babe," Stella points out.

"First of all, that is so lame. Second, that's not fair to add because *obviously* you'll do that one." She shrugs smugly, and I rack my brain for anything she hates. "Okay, then we're adding 'Blow Santa.'"

"What? Disgusting." She gasps. "His balls must be so sweaty in that costume."

"Sorry, *I* don't make the rules," I mock.

"Evil." She glares. "You know my gag reflex sucks."

We finish it up, and I have to admit, this looks like the ultimate holiday list for a little fun. Of the sugar *and* spice variety.

Merry Mischief List

- [ ] Build a snowman
- [ ] Ice skating
- [ ] Snowball Fight
- [ ] Kiss Under Mistletoe
- [ ] Drink spiked hot chocolate
- [ ] Decorate a Christmas tree
- [ ] Triple gumdrop tower ~~Gingerbread man (or woman) tower~~
- [ ] Bake gingerbread man cookies (XLGD)
- [ ] Block Olivia
- [ ] Blow Santa
- [ ] Elf lick whipped cream off ~~tits~~
- [ ] Snow angels

Loser gets naked at Desert Bowl

7

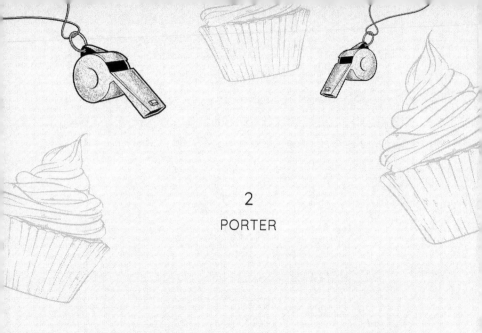

2
PORTER

"For crying out loud," I mutter to myself. We're two weeks away from the Desert Bowl in Arizona, one of the biggest college football games of the year, and the guys are playing like it's tryouts.

My smart watch buzzes, pulling my attention from the practice field. It's yet *another* weather alert about the snowstorm sweeping across the Northeast. It'll be a damn miracle if I'm able to fly out to New Jersey tonight before everything is shut down. *Then again... if I got stuck here in Florida, I would have more time to prepare for this bowl game.*

"Heads up, Coach!"

I look just in time to catch a football torpedoing towards my face. Gripping the ball tightly, I lower it to my side while looking for the player who threw it.

"Caruso!" I shout at my starting quarterback and team captain, Noah Caruso.

"Yes, Coach," Noah says, taking off his helmet and joining me on the sideline. "Sorry, sir."

"What the hell is going on out there?" I ask, throwing an arm out towards the field.

"Honestly..." He shakes his head. "I think everyone's a bit antsy about break. I know it's not an excuse but—"

I lift a hand, cutting him off, and blow my whistle. "Huddle up," I shout, and the whole team gathers around me. They're dripping in sweat, huffing like hippos, and seem completely worn out.

Have I been pushing them too hard?

This is the second week in a row of our two-a-day practices...

"I know you're all itching to get out of here and head home for the holidays," I say loud enough for them all to hear. "But I'm not letting you walk off this field today looking like the fucking Pee Wee football team. You're better than this. We haven't gotten so far this season by acting like a bunch of toddlers in grown men's bodies, now have we?" No one replies. "I said, have we?"

"No, Coach," they say in unison.

"So shake off whatever bullshit is keeping you from playing like the seasoned athletes I know you are." I fold my arms across my chest. "Noah, you're gonna sit a few out. Anderson, you're up."

"Yes, Coach," Elijah Anderson, our backup quarterback, says eagerly.

"Now go out there and show me you deserve to win this damn Desert Bowl!"

"Yes, Coach!" the team shouts.

"Okay, bring it in," I say, putting my hand in the middle, and they follow suit.

"Stingrays on three," Noah shouts. "One, two—"

"Stingrays!"

The guys run back out, setting up on the line of scrimmage, and the ball is hiked to Anderson. He's protected by the offensive linemen, and within seconds, the ball is spiraling downfield towards running back Theo Schroeder. He catches the ball, leaves the defenders in the dust, and scores a touchdown.

"Thank you!" I shout while jogging down the sidelines towards them. "That's what I want. Now do it again! And any defenseman that lets Theo get away from them will be doing suicides for the last ten minutes of practice."

3

ANDI

"Sorry again," Theo says as we wait anxiously in line at Tampa airport security. He and Stella are about thirty minutes away from missing their flight but luckily, mine boards a bit later. "I swear I wanted to leave earlier, but Coach Porter was riding us harder than Santa rides his sleigh."

"Why must someone so hot be such a hardass?" Stella says as we finally arrive at the front of the line and place our stuff on the conveyor belt. "Such a disappointment."

"Yeah, he totally killed my pre-holiday buzz," Theo says before passing through the metal detector.

"Pretty sure your pre-holiday buzz will be firmly fixed by the time you land," I say, passing through after him.

"Yeah," Stella chimes in, joining us to wait for our bags. "Thanks to Daddy Schroeder, we'll be drinking expensive champagne all the way to Denver."

"Please stop referring to my father that way," Theo groans.

"Well, once *you* start paying for our upgrades instead of *Daddy* Schroeder, I will." Stella winks. They've been casually sleeping together since last year, and Theo's dick seems to be the gift that keeps on giving.

"Next year, I'm coming with you guys," I say, fully aware my parents would never let me live it down if I missed Christmas for a ski trip.

"The more the merrier," Theo says, pulling me in and kissing my cheek.

"Excuse me," a security agent says, grabbing our attention. "Is this bag one of yours?" He gestures to the black backpack which, of course, belongs to Theo.

"Really, bro?" I say. "Did you forget to take your testosterone injections out?"

"Ha ha," Theo says, narrowing his eyes on me before turning his attention to the security officer. "That's mine, sir."

Every time Theo turns on his preppy rich boy manners, it cracks me up.

"Please come here as I take a look through it," the officer instructs.

Theo heads over while Stella and I wait a few steps back. The officer shuffles the bag around for a few minutes, then pulls out a tiny bottle and turns his amused gaze to Theo.

"Next time, please remove the lube from your bag and include it with your separated liquids, sir," the officer says, handing Theo back his things.

"Sorry, won't happen again," Theo replies, repacking his bag.

"Seriously?" Stella asks him. "Pretty sure they sell lube in Colorado."

"Just wanted to make sure we were prepared for the triple

gumdrop," Theo tells Stella, throwing an arm over her shoulder as we walk toward our gates. "You know, in case we gotta lube up your ass?"

"No one will be going *near* my ass, thank you very much!" Stella declares, shoving him off. "Maybe we'll need it for *yours.*"

"Hey." Theo throws his hands up. "I'm comfortable with my masculinity. I'd be willing to take a peg for the team."

I freeze in place. "Excuse me, the *team*? I thought this was Battle of the Bitches. A vs. S. The hoedown showdown."

"We never said help couldn't be enlisted," Stella points out.

"Yeah, but you're going to *Tits on Ice* with Theo, and I'm visiting *family!*" I snap. "Who should I enlist? My cousins? What is this, *Bates Motel?*"

"Calm down, I didn't mean for you to go full Judge Judy," she grumbles.

"You know..." Theo says, throwing his arm over my shoulder. "We can head to the family restroom and knock the triple gumdrop off *both* your lists."

I grin up at his handsome, hopeful face. "As *life-changing* as that sounds, I don't think Stella rolls both ways."

Stella snakes an arm around my waist and kisses my cheek. "With you, Andi-kins? I might be in."

"Oh, hell yes." Theo grins appreciatively. "Let's get—"

"This is the final boarding call for Flight AH263 to Denver. Please proceed to gate 43."

"No!" Theo groans. "I will literally pay someone to delay this flight."

"Sorry, buddy." I laugh, patting his chest. "No airport gumdrops for you."

"A tragedy, really," he replies.

"Well, have a safe flight," Stella says, giving me a big hug. "And you're going down, baby."

"Yes, yes, I am... on Santa." I wink, feeling confident since she and I both know that's more than likely the one item she'll skip.

"Don't worry," Theo says, hugging me goodbye. "I'm sure Arizona won't be *that* cold in the middle of winter."

"Yeah, yeah, game on, losers."

I wander the terminal, hunting for my winter guilty pleasure. After I've finally got a peppermint mocha cupcake securely stored for later, I find my gate and settle in. Pulling out my phone, I fight the urge to open up social media but ultimately cave, as always.

A picture of my friend Charlie and her shithead boyfriend, Jonathan, wearing Santa hats fills the screen. *When is she gonna realize what a tool bag he is?* I scroll down to another of my old fling Elijah and his new bombshell of a girlfriend petting a horse on his family ranch. Things ending between me and him were so much simpler than the shit show with Olivia.

And as if I summoned her myself, Olivia's smiling face fills the screen as—*what the hell?*

Another girl's lips are planted firmly on her cheek paired with the caption: *Up to snow good.*

Wow, Olivia. You're texting me like I'm Jack Frost, but you've already clearly moved on.

A notification from my airline's app comes on the screen.

Flight AA329 to Richmond International Airport has been canceled. Please contact customer service for information regarding the next available flight.

"Motherfucker."

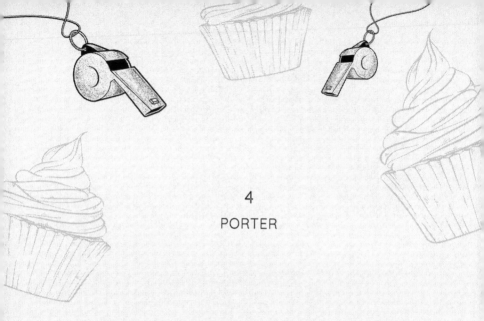

4

PORTER

> Flight EH489 to Atlantic City International
> has been canceled. Please contact
> customer service for information regarding
> the next available flight.

A whoosh of relief leaves me, immediately replaced by a pressing guilt in my stomach.

I'm such a selfish asshole.

Gathering my things, I pop in a headphone, dial Mom's number, and make my way to the exit.

"Let me guess," she says, disappointed. "Flight's been canceled?"

"Wow, Mom. You have a bug placed in the Tampa airport or something? I *just* got the notification." *Not that I wasn't expecting it.*

"No, but I do watch the Weather Channel and was hoping your flight would get in before they shut the airports down for the next few days."

"Me too," I say, hoping to sound more convincing than I feel.

"If you weren't such a workaholic, I *might* actually believe you, Jimmy." I chuckle at her use of the nickname—the one she's been using since before I started football and was called exclusively by my last name. "Just promise me you won't spend the entire holiday locked in your lonely, empty office rewatching the same players' film and worrying about the bowl game."

"The boys are depending on me—"

"And who are you depending on?" she cuts me off.

"I have Knox. You know he's always there for me."

"I know. We just really miss you. And listen, honey, I know being head coach puts a lot of pressure on you, but we all believe in you."

"Just trying not to screw it up," I mumble.

"Don't worry. I'm sure it'll be a *super* bowl game, honey," she says, and I can't help but laugh, struggling to remember the last time we got through a phone call without some type of football or sports-related pun.

Like an oasis in the desert, a bar appears before me. A stiff drink sounds like the perfect remedy for the guilt filling me from this conversation. There's an open seat next to a leggy brunette, and, given my only other choice is a guy who's literally fallen asleep on the bar, it seems like a no-brainer.

"I know, you're right," I tell Mom, settling on the bar stool.

"Thank you. So please try to have some *actual* fun. Your x's and o's will still be there come December twenty-seventh."

"Okay, Mom. I'll try to have some *actual* fun." The bartender walks up, and I pull the phone from my ear. "Bourbon, neat, please."

"You got it," he says before walking away.

"Alright, well, I'm gonna let you go, Jimmy," Mom says.

"Okay, love you."

"Love you," she replies and hangs up, allowing me to mull over my next week's plans—or rather, lack thereof—in peace.

The brunette spins her seat toward me, her leg brushing mine as she glares at me with a familiar face I can't *quite* place.

"Well, if it isn't Mr. Buzzkill," she says mockingly before taking a long sip of the sangria in her hand.

"Excuse me?" I scoff.

"Come to give me a detention, Coach Porter?" She bumps her wrists together, fists clenched. "Cuff me now, and let's get it over with."

Pretty sure I'd remember tying this girl up... *Or have I really slept with so many people I can't remember their names anymore?*

"I'm sorry, do we know each other?" I ask.

An incredulous laugh rips from her. "Well, I suppose I shouldn't be surprised you have no clue who I am." She spins away, nursing another long pull from her glass. Her cheeks are flushed, and I'd wager my year's salary it's not her first of the night.

The bartender places my drink down, but I can't stop analyzing her face. The way her eyelashes flutter every time she pretends not to glance at me. How her lips roll together as she fights to make another confusing assumption. She shifts in her seat, and my attention drops to her long legs wrapped around each other.

I'd rather they were wrapped around me.

"I've seen you almost every day at the practice stadium for the last three years," she blurts.

"Only football players and—" My eyes drop to her Crystal Bay University Cheer tank top.

"Cheerleaders," she finishes for me. "Yep, that's me."

Great, I was fantasizing about a student. Head Coach of the Year... "I only pay attention to my players."

"You also dated my sister," she supplies.

"What?" I all but break my neck turning to look at her. The only legitimate ex I've had in years is Jess Lyons, and she has a younger sister, but the only thing I remember about her is she was obsessed with cupcakes and was hardly a teenager.

Yeah, six years ago, you dumbass. Do the math.

"*You're* Cupcake?" I ask, eyes tracing her face for any similarities to my ex. If they *are* related, they look drastically different aside from matching brown eyes.

"I'm sorry?" She fights a laugh. "I'm who?"

"You're *Jess's* sister?"

"Andi Lyons, at your service." She eyes me curiously. "Cupcake?"

I roll my lips together. "Yeah, the only thing I remember about you is that you had an obsession with cupcakes."

"It was not an obsession! I like cupcakes a very *normal* amount," she argues, throwing a hand over her heart. My eyes follow the movement, locking in on her chest. Her perfectly symmetrical chest... *What the hell is wrong with me?*

"If you say so," I reply, forcing my gaze toward her mouth as she takes another sip of the sangria. "Are you even old enough to drink?"

"Seriously?" She glares at me. "I'm twenty-one. Do you need to see my ID?"

"I'll take your word for it," I say, feeling absolutely ancient.

"Good." She swirls the liquid in her glass. "Your flight get canceled too?"

"Yep," I say and take a sip of my drink. "Were you able to reschedule?"

"Nope," she clips. "Next flight isn't till Christmas Eve, and by then it's not worth it since we have to be back by the twenty-seventh for practice. You?"

"Yeah, same boat," I say, as if I even tried to find an alternative flight.

"Merry freaking Christmas." She slants her drink towards me, and we clink glasses.

"Any of your family still down here?" I ask, knowing Jess always raved about her holidays at their vacation cabin in Virginia.

"Nope. They all flew out earlier this week."

"That's too bad."

She orders another glass, and I consider asking for my check to get the hell out of here, but for some unknown reason I stay.

"Any friends who stayed on campus for the holidays?" I ask.

"Not a single one," she replies. "I was seeing this girl, but last week I dumped her in the middle of Salty Pete's after she wouldn't stop accusing me of being an attention whore because I like to have a good time. I mean, what's the point of going out if you can't let loose and shake your ass on the dance floor? Is it my fault she sits in the corner like a bump on a log?" I fight a smile at her information dump. "She said I'm exclusively 'fuck buddy' material because all I want to do is go out or get it on. But what's wrong with that? There's no shame in having a good time or liking sex! Who wouldn't want to have orgasms daily? It's like a basic human right." She stares at me intently, and I struggle to determine whether or not it was a rhetorical question. Either way, I have no answer.

"I mean," she continues, "is there really something so wrong about rolling with the vibes of wherever we're at? If we go out, I'm gonna have a good time. If we go to the beach, I'm gonna relax and enjoy some fun in the sun. If we fuck, I'm gonna make sure we both come till we see stars!" *I'm struggling to see the problem here.* "Does that really make me such a monster?"

"I'm sure you're a very nice person," I say, still attempting to move past the details of her clearly very satisfying sex life. Details I shouldn't know or be focusing on.

"Well, *thank you,* person who forgot I exist," she replies, pulling me back to the present.

"I know everything seems super messed up right now." I swirl my drink. "But it'll get better."

Andi's eyes slide to mine, the same color as the liquor in my glass. "Are you Dr. Phil'ing me?"

"I'm surprised you know who he is," I tease.

"I may be young, but I'm not *that* young. I grew up watching Dr. Phil, Jerry Springer, and Maury like the rest of 'em."

"Okay, okay." I laugh. "I get your point."

"How am I supposed to deck the halls in these conditions? We're in the most humid, un-festive place on Earth. I was really looking forward to going full Buddy the Elf." She drops her face against her hand and groans. "The snow. The cabin decorated top to bottom. All of it... magic. The only positive to any of this," she slurs, tipping her glass toward me, "is I don't have to hear how freaking *fantastic* Jess's perfect life is." Her mention of Jess catches me off guard.

"So sorry you and your fuck buddy broke up," she sasses in a high-pitched impersonation, assumedly of her sister. "When I met my pro-football-playing husband, Devon, I knew it was right. Someday you'll meet someone and just know." She huffs a laugh, returning to her normal pitch.

Wow, this conversation is an absolute dumpster fire.

"The only thing she knew was how much his status in the NFL would help her climb the professional ladder," she scoffs. "Who wouldn't want to hire the wife of a pro athlete to be a sports reporter? They know she can get an inside scoop to half the team by proximity alone." Andi's eyes widen, mouth parting open. "Shit. I'm sorry, that was super insensitive of me. And Devon's really not that great."

"He *is* great," I say, smirking, thinking of one of my old teammates from Tampa. Sure, it hurt how things went down with Jess, but I'm not gonna mope over her for the rest of my life. And Andi's right. Jess was too busy chasing the next story to give a shit about her personal life... or me.

"Ugh, yeah, he really is. Still, sorry for bringing her up."

"It's ancient history," I say, waving her off. Partly to make her feel better but mostly because it's the truth.

"You guys mind cashing out?" the bartender asks. "We're switching servers."

"Aww, you're leaving us, Mr. Bartender Man?" Andi grumbles.

"It's fine," I tell her. "We should probably get out of here anyway. It's getting late." *And she definitely shouldn't have another drink, that's for sure.*

"Fine," she concedes with a huff. "Put the buzzkill's drink on my tab."

"Absolutely not," I say, reaching for my wallet.

Andi places her hand on my forearm, soft brown eyes boring into mine. A breath catches in my throat, and I swallow it down. "I just drunk vented to you about our exes. It's the least I can do," she argues.

"How about *I* pay for *your* drink as an apology for my lack of advice?" I counter.

"How about *I* pay and you forget every embarrassing thing I said?"

If I've learned anything in life, it's not to argue with a drunk, sad, determined woman. I put my hands up, signaling a forfeit. "Deal."

She cashes out, and we make our way towards the exit.

"You drive here?" I ask, attempting to mask my concern considering she clearly can't operate a vehicle in this condition.

"Nope. Didn't intend on needing a ride until a week from now," she huffs, then releases a soft laugh. "Well, not *that* kind of ride, anyway."

I choose to ignore her sexual innuendo and glance towards the taxi bay at the variety of men waiting for a new fare. Two headlines flash before my eyes.

Student Murdered By Taxi Driver After Being Abandoned By CBU's Head Coach At Tampa International Airport. Why Was He Too Busy to Give Her A Ride?

Or the alternative...

CBU Head Coach Takes Home Drunk Student. Which Head Was He Thinking With?

I decide the one where Andi doesn't end up in a ditch somewhere seems to be the better alternative.

"I'll take you home," I say.

She eyes me skeptically. "It's fine. I'll take an Uber."

Student Murdered by Uber Driver...

"It's really no problem," I assure her. "I'm heading back that way anyways." *Liar.*

It's not like she knows where I live. When I got the job at CBU, I decided to keep my place in Tampa since the commute is perfectly reasonable. It's actually my favorite part of the day. A half hour with whatever audiobook I'm listening to and no one bothering me. *Heaven.* It also allows me to keep my work and private life as separate as possible. No head coach wants to run into players every time they go to dinner or the grocery store.

Andi clutches her small carry-on, swaying back and forth on her heels. "Fine. I guess you can give me a ride."

We start towards the parking garage, and she stumbles over the curb. I throw my arm out, catching her seconds before she face-plants onto the concrete.

"Okay, Cupcake," I say, hooking her arm around my waist as I grab her bags. "Hold on to me so we don't end up having to take you to the hospital instead of your dorm."

"Whatever, buzzkill," she groans.

We finally arrive at my car, and I help Andi into the

passenger seat before putting our things in the trunk. I hop in the driver's side, and she's already leaned the chair back, making herself at home and looking completely relaxed. Like she belongs there.

Andi spends a few minutes going through the radio stations as I pull us onto the dark highway, and then she relaxes into the seat, humming some Christmas song by Michael Bublé. *Why does this bring me a sense of relief?* She's a far cry from the stressed-out woman at the bar. *The stressed-out woman who's your ex's younger sister.* I grip the steering wheel, cursing myself for relishing in her comfort.

"So what are you gonna do now?" I ask after a few minutes of silence.

I'm about to repeat the question when a loud snorting sound fills the small space. My eyes swing briefly from the road to Andi, and not only has she fallen asleep, but she's fully snoring. If I didn't know any better, I'd think Piglet's taken up residence on my passenger seat. I attempt to wake her, but she doesn't budge. I quickly realize the pitcher of sangria might have been a bit too much, even for her tall, muscular body to tolerate.

"Andi…" I say louder, shaking her shoulder. Not even a single movement.

Shit.

After a few more failed attempts to wake her up, I pull into a rest area, cursing myself for not asking where she lived as soon as we got in the car.

It's seven a.m., and I've already had my morning protein shake, run three miles, done today's weight training, listened to an hour of my audiobook, and now I'm dialing the one person I talk to whenever I've done anything remotely interesting. He picks up on the third ring.

"I know I said call anytime… but seven a.m.? That's kinda pushing it," he grumbles as if he hasn't already completed the same morning routine. Minus the audiobook because he claims actually *reading* a book is better for the mind.

"There's a cheerleader in my bed…" I say, glancing in my bedroom at Andi.

"One of mine?" he asks, referring to the Tampa Bay Barracudas cheerleaders from the NFL team he plays on. The team where we played together before I had a career-ending injury after only five years on the job.

"Nope…" Silence fills the air. "One of mine."

"Back up. You slept with a *college* cheerleader and didn't invite me?"

"I never said I slept with her," I whisper, shutting the bedroom door. The next ten minutes consist of me filling him in on the airport bar run-in down to her passing out in my car.

"Damn, man," Knox says once I'm done. "And your first instinct was 'I'll bring my ex's sister back to my place'?"

"Well, it was that or leave her in front of a random dorm on campus, which didn't seem to be a particularly appealing option."

"Is she hotter than Jess?"

Exponentially. "Really, man?"

"Sorry," he says half-heartedly as a laugh comes through the line. "So what's she like?"

"All I know is she's a cheerleader for CBU, has an unhealthy obsession with cupcakes, and, apparently, sangria is a truth serum for her because I got her whole life story last night."

"She got a free Porter therapy session, and you didn't even get laid? What a gentleman," he mocks.

"She's Jess's sister... *and* a student."

"Since when are you opposed to a good time?"

"Did you not hear me say she's Jess's *sister*?" I ask. "And even *more* importantly, a CBU student. That simple fact alone could derail my entire career."

"Excuses, excuses. I say tap that."

I pull eggs out of the fridge to start breakfast. "And that's why I don't take advice from the guy who buys his condoms from *Costco*. Who needs a hundred-and-thirty-two-pack?"

"It's cost effective!" Knox counters.

"Listen, I gotta go. I'll call you later."

"Unless the story gets better, don't."

5

ANDI

The scent of fresh sheets and something innately masculine, combined with a pounding headache, overwhelms my senses.

"Ugh," I groan, taking another deep inhale through my nose.

Hold up. My bed does not smell like a Dior warehouse.

I snap my head up, taking in my surroundings. Wherever I am, this place is freaking swanky. There's a walk-in closet full of suits, an ensuite bathroom, and completely modern furniture around the room, with a massive flat screen taking up almost the entire damn wall.

I blink everything into focus, attempting to conjure up last night's memories. The last thing I remember, I was at the airport bar, wallowing in self-pity and talking to—

Panic courses through me, and I bolt out of the bed. My muscles instantly relax upon discovering I'm still fully clothed—sans shoes.

I'm ninety percent sure we didn't sleep together given I

woke up dressed and alone. *Or maybe he's not a cuddler, and I was cold?*

My eyes are glued to the bed as I try to place together the puzzle pieces of how I ended up in what I'm assuming is Porter's bedroom.

Maybe I can leave without him noticing me. It wouldn't be the first time I slipped out after a hookup. Not because I was ashamed, but because that was all they were: hookups. I never felt the need to stay and do the whole *wanna talk about it over brunch?* thing.

I tiptoe over to the door and gently place my hand on the knob, pausing to hear if there's any movement on the other side.

There's a brief shuffle, and the door swings open, directly into my face.

"Oww!" I shout, bringing my hands up to my nose as the pounding in my head triples.

"Oh my god," Porter gasps, peeking his head around the door. "I'm so sorry. Are you okay?"

"Fantastic. I've always wanted a nose job, so thanks for saving me the money," I deadpan, opening the door wide and brushing past him to dart down the stairs. His footsteps echo behind me, and I choose to ignore them. I slow my pace towards the front door, where my carry-on bag and purse are sitting. Everything perfectly in place for my inevitable getaway.

"I made breakfast," he says as I continue towards my things.

"No thanks, I've gotta…" I pause, trying to figure out what excuse I can possibly give considering he and I both know I don't have anywhere to be. "Go."

"Okay."

I pause and turn to face him. "Did um... we sleep together last night?"

"Sleep, as in?" An amused smile crosses his face.

"Did we have sex?" I clarify to leave no room for misinterpretation.

"I don't sleep with students, and..." He trails off, eyes roaming me disapprovingly from head to toes. "You're also Jess's kid sister."

Kid sister?!

"Right." I nod my head, heat flushing my cheeks in embarrassment and anger. "Well, I guess I better go find a school bus to hop on."

I reach for my purse and, in my rush, knock it to the ground. All the contents are scattered out on his spotless wood floors, and he rushes over, helping me repack. "I've got it."

"I don't mind." He extends a hand towards me with my little box from the airport. "Wouldn't want you to forget your emergency cupcake," he says, a smug grin on his lips.

Oh, good god. He'll never let that go now.

I snatch the container from his hand and shove the remaining items in my bag before standing up. "Thanks."

He eyes me amusingly before folding his thick arms across his chest. It's the same damn thing he does when the boys are out on the field, and he looks even sexier now his attention is fixated on me. He's wearing athletic shorts and a tight T-shirt that fits him like a second skin. *Ugh, stop being so damn hot.*

"Andi?" Porter says, snapping me out of my ogling.

"Yeah!" I resituate the purse on my shoulder and grab the

handle of my carry-on. "Thanks for..." I glance toward the stairs to his bedroom. "Letting me crash. Better get home before I miss curfew." I run out and down the steps of his front porch onto the sidewalk of what appears to be a bougie neighborhood of townhomes.

Where the hell am I?

Taking a deep breath, I pull out my phone, opening the Uber app. My foot bounces impatiently as I type in the address for my place, and the screen goes black.

Excuse me, what the hell?

I press the side button, and as if this morning couldn't get any worse, my damn phone is dead.

"Of course," I groan, shoving it back in my purse. *Where the hell am I? How am I gonna get back to campus?*

Embarrassment settles into my bones as I realize there's only one option that doesn't leave me flat broke or on public transportation for the next several hours.

I turn around slowly, and that same smug grin awaits me with the door propped open and a cup of coffee in his hands. My pride *almost* has me turning back around and bolting in the opposite direction, but the raging hangover is begging me to suck it up.

I drag myself back to the front porch, and Porter's annoyingly arrogant smile only grows.

"Forget something?" he mocks.

"Well..." I clear my throat, hands on my hips. "Considering you *kidnapped* me and apparently live in—well, to be honest, I have no idea where we are."

"Near downtown Tampa," he says over the brim of his coffee cup.

"Wonderful. As I was saying, considering you kidnapped

me to your swanky townhouse near downtown Tampa, could you give me a ride back to CBU?"

"What happened to the school bus?"

"Turns out the route doesn't pass by the devil's house." I shrug. "Safety precaution."

"To be fair, I tried to give you a ride home last night, and you passed out in my car."

"It was a long day."

"Anyone ever told you that you snore like an F1 race car?"

My mouth falls open. "Never mind, I think I'll walk. If I leave now, I should make it there by Christmas."

I spin around, and a deep laugh fills the air seconds before loud steps sound and a warm hand lands on my elbow. "Come on," he says in a soothing tone I've never heard from him before. "Eat breakfast. Then I'll give you a ride."

"I'm not hungry," I lie. My stomach actually curses at me when the words leave my mouth.

"It'll help the hangover," Porter argues, raising his brows. His thumb brushes lightly over my arm, and I struggle to find another suitable excuse.

"I'll just eat the cupcake." I smile sweetly. "It is for emergencies, after all."

"I already cooked. Don't make me waste a perfectly good plate of sausage and eggs," he says. *Damn, that does sound good.* "Save your cupcake for later."

"Fine," I concede, brushing past him. "I'll eat your damn sausage."

"So, are you disappointed you can't get up north?" Porter asks as we partake in a round of small talk on the drive to CBU. My stomach is full, and although I'll never admit it, my hangover is *slightly* less intense.

"On a scale of one to ten, ten being the most disappointed, I'd say I'm a hard eleven. A white Christmas is basically all I dream of every year. The cabin is a winter paradise compared to our hellscape."

"Most people would consider *this*"—he waves a hand at the palm trees passing by and the blue sky overhead—"paradise."

I lean back in the seat and take in our surroundings. "True. It's just, Christmas doesn't feel like Christmas without snow and the lights and the vibes."

"The vibes?"

"Yeah, you know. The old red pickup truck carrying a snow-covered tree on a postcard kind of vibes?"

"That's a very specific description."

"It's a very specific vibe," I counter.

"Well, why can't you have those here?" he asks, and I wave a hand at the surroundings like he did moments before. "Oh, come on. Sunshine and blue skies don't ruin the vibes of Christmas. *You* make the vibes, they don't make you."

I choke on a laugh. "Wow, how Coachella of you."

"I'm thirty-one, not a hundred and one. I'm in tune with the *vibes*... I've also been to Coachella."

"Of course you have. Still"—I hold up a hand—"please

stop using the word 'vibes.' Say 'atmosphere' or 'ambiance' or something more… your century."

He scowls at me, and I glance out the window to resist admiring the way his arm muscles flex each time he readjusts his grip on the steering wheel.

"So…" he says, tapping the dark leather. "You gonna block Olivia?"

My head whips so fast in his direction it makes my neck ache. "I'm sorry, what?"

"I asked if you're gonna block Olivia."

Did I tell him about the list?

Or only about Olivia?

"How did you? Why would? That's—" I stutter as I readjust myself in the seat while he stares at me in amusement. "You know what? New rule. No more talking. This is a silent Uber."

"A silent Uber?"

"Yeah, you know? With Uber, if you don't wanna talk to the driver, you can choose the 'silent' ride. And they leave you the hell alone. And definitely don't ask questions about your ex."

"Oh, *now* you don't want to talk about exes? Is that exclusively a sangria subject?"

"Silent. Uber," I repeat, desperate to end this conversation. Porter apparently follows directions well as a quietness falls over the cab of the vehicle. I fight every intrusive thought begging me to fill the silence and turn up the radio instead.

A few minutes later—minutes that felt like hours—we pull up to the curb of my dorm at CBU. "Thanks for the ride," I say, hopping out of the vehicle. He follows my lead, meeting me at the back of the Range Rover, and opens the trunk to retrieve my bag. "And thanks for doing your professional duty of making sure I didn't sleep on the airport floor last night."

"Welcome," he says, folding those damn muscular arms over his chest. Like he knows it makes him look intimidating and sexy as all hell. *Arrogant prick.* "Bye, Andi."

"Bye, Coach."

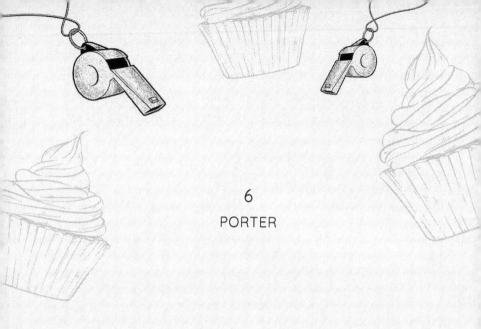

6
PORTER

Rubbing my eyes, I see the tape of our last game come back into focus. I've spent the last five hours trying to analyze how to improve our chances of winning the bowl game on New Year's Eve. We've got a talented group of players this year and have won most of our games, but the competitive spirit in me wants to win them all. That's the only way we'll ever be able to make it to a national championship. Which is pretty much the career goal for a college coach. If you can win a championship, *maybe* you'll get moved up to coach professional someday. And much like the guys I'm coaching, there's not much I wouldn't give to be back on an NFL field come game day. *Even if it's as a coach instead of a player.*

After watching the same clip eight times and being unable to focus, I call it a day. I'm not even supposed to be working, but I needed a distraction when Andi blasted off faster than Max Verstappen.

There was something uncomfortably normal about having her in my space. For the first time since my accident, an interruption to my routine felt welcome rather than feared. *A bit ironic considering the reason for it.*

I unfold the small list she dropped at my house this morning and examine it for the twentieth time today.

Block Olivia

Blow Santa

Elf lick whipped cream off tits

A smile breaks free as I put it back in my pocket and leave my office. With everyone on vacation, the practice building is empty and eerily quiet.

Leave it to the workaholic to be the only one here.

I exit the vacant building into the sunshine and warm Florida air. A pleasant reminder I won't have to spend the next week in the cold, arctic tundra of New Jersey. Unlike Andi, I'd much rather have sunshine than snowflakes for Christmas.

Hopping in my Range Rover, I start a podcast before pulling out of the staff lot. I force myself to fully focus on the work/life balance episode, a topic especially targeted at people like me who struggle to maintain boundaries around the holidays.

"It's important to allow yourself time to decompress from the hard work you have completed this past year. With the new year will come new beginnings, new opportunities for growth, new ideas for how to efficiently run your business and hold a clear mind. If you don't give yourself time away from your tasks, you will be unable to see them in a new light."

Hard to step away from your job when there're hundreds of players and staff who contribute to the season, along with tens of thousands of adoring fans, relying on you.

"Don't see the holiday festivities as distractions, but rather a break that will allow you to come back refreshed with a new perspective. It is imperative—"

A flash of something comes into the road a few yards ahead, and I slam on the brakes. Whatever, or whoever, it was must have been bumped by the car and be on the ground considering I no longer see them.

"Shit," I mutter to myself, jumping out to round the front. "Are you o—" I pause in my tracks, looking down at furious and familiar amber eyes.

"Did you seriously just hit me with your car?" Andi snaps, glaring up at me.

"Are you okay?" I grab her elbow and pull her to her feet. Once standing, she yanks her arm out of my grasp, placing her hands firmly on her hips. Sweat drips down her body, which is covered by nothing but a tight sports bra and athletic shorts, making her legs look a mile long.

"No, I'm not okay!" She throws her arms up incredulously. "You *hit* me with your *fucking* car!"

"I'm sorry, you came out of nowhere."

"*I* came out of nowhere?" she scoffs. "So now it's *my* fault you don't look where you're driving? I was running on the *sidewalk*. You're the one who rolled through a stop sign." I glance around and sure as shit, she's right. I was so in my head I ignored the stop sign where the parking lot leads to the main road. Andi winces and reaches down to her knee, which is covered in blood.

I don't think this is what Knox had in mind when he said "tap that."

"Let me park," I say, pointing towards my car. "I've got a first aid kit in the back to clean you up."

"I'll be fine. It's just a little"—she glances down—"a lot of blood."

"Seriously?" I raise my brows. "You're gonna risk scarring because you're too stubborn to let me help you?"

She lets out a huff of defeat. "Fine."

After parking the car, I round to the back, and pop open the trunk, gesturing for her to sit on the edge. Inside the first aid kit, I retrieve a few antiseptic wipes and a large bandage. Taking her ankle, I place the sole of her tennis shoe against my thigh to get a better angle. "I'm gonna clean the dirt and blood off. Make sure there's nothing else stuck in there."

"Sure, whatever," she huffs.

Using a bottle of water, I wet a towel and gently drag it against her skin. Given our proximity, her sweet smell distracts me as I try to focus on the task at hand. After the wound is mostly clean, I rip open the package for the antiseptic. "This next part may sting a little."

"I think I can handle a little—" Her smart remark turns into a hiss, and she grips my forearm, nails digging in. I enjoy it a little too much.

"You good?"

"Yeah." She releases a breath, along with my arm. "I'm fine."

"All done," I say, glancing into her brown eyes already fixated on mine. There's a little fleck of gold in her right eye, and I find myself mesmerized by it. *Why is she so distracting?*

"Thanks." She fights a smile as a pause beats between us. "Why did you ask me about blocking Olivia?"

"Seemed like the easiest thing to mark off that list of yours," I admit as it burns a hole in my back pocket.

Her eyes go wide, lips parting. "What–what do you mean?" I slide the paper out, holding it with two fingers before her, and she snatches it. "How did you get this? Did you go through my stuff last night?"

"Whoa, whoa." I throw up my hands. "*You* dropped it when bolting out of my house this morning."

"And you just *forgot* to give it to me?"

I shrug. "I would've when I dropped you off earlier, but you, again, bolted."

"Well, it doesn't matter. I'm not doing it anymore anyways."

"Why not?"

"Um, you read the whole thing, right? It's pretty much how to have the perfect winter wonderland Christmas, and in case you forgot"—she waves her arms around exaggeratedly —"we're in Florida. Aka the place Santa goes *after* he's delivered all the presents to drink a piña colada and work on his sunburn."

"So you're just gonna quit because of a little warm weather?"

"A lot of warm weather," she corrects.

I cross my arms over my chest and raise a challenging brow at her. "I didn't peg you as a quitter. Especially when a fun time is involved."

She mirrors my stance. "And I didn't peg you as the type of guy who knows what actually classifies as a good time."

"I have layers."

"Like an ogre."

"You mean like an onion?"

"No. I'm going with the *Shrek* thing."

I narrow my eyes at her. "Smartass."

The hidden look of disappointment on her face makes me uncomfortable.

"What if I help you with one of them?" I say, knowing there's an item on the list she may need assistance with given our location.

"Do I get to choose?" she asks, waggling her eyebrows.

I immediately recall the more mischievous items, then mentally slap myself for even allowing my mind to wander there. *She's Jess's sister. Remember?*

"No," I say, redirecting my train of thought. "Consider it an apology for hitting you with my car."

"I guess you do owe me," she concedes. "What do you have in mind?"

7

ANDI

"Okay, now *this* is badass," I say with a huge grin as we walk into the empty hockey arena at Crystal Bay University. The temperature has plummeted from outside, and we quickly put on our jackets.

"What size shoe are you?" Porter asks, walking towards a supply closet.

"Eight and a half." He disappears inside and emerges with two sets of ice skates. "You don't have to do it with me. Wouldn't want you dislocating a hip or something, old man."

"Hah, hilarious," he says, narrowing his eyes at me. "But why should you get to have all the fun? Besides, someone's gotta keep you from busting your ass on the ice."

"Is that so?" I bark out a laugh. "And what makes you think I don't know how to skate?"

"You're a Florida girl." He smiles smugly. "Need I say more?"

"Mm-hmm, we'll see."

We lace up our skates, and I'm trembling both from the

cold but also the excitement to get out on that perfectly smooth ice and prove Mr. Smug Face wrong. He opens the door and gestures for me to step out onto the rink first. I purposefully struggle, giving the full giraffe-on-roller skates show, and while it may look ridiculous, Porter's deep laugh echoing through the empty arena makes it worth it.

"Told you," he taunts. "It's harder than it looks."

"Well, maybe if I just..." I do a little shimmy, then stand up straight before taking off at full speed. I dig my toe into the ice, then push my body off the ground and do a single axel before landing perfectly. I glide around, then skid to a stop, and Porter has a look of pure shock on his face. "Not bad for a Florida girl, huh?"

"Where the hell did you learn to do that?" he asks, skating over to me.

"There's a pond behind our cabin in Virginia that freezes over in winter. It's where I spend pretty much every waking minute."

"You taught *yourself*?"

"What, like it's hard?" I wink, maintaining eye contact as I skate away backwards. He catches up easily, and we take turns "showing off" our skills around the rink.

"Wanna try something a bit more difficult?" Porter asks after we've sufficiently warmed up.

"I'm always down for a challenge," I say as he glides away, coming to a stop in the middle of the rink.

"Skate towards me, and as soon as you're within reach, jump with your hands straight up."

"Excuse me?" I scoff. "You want me to *what* now?"

"Trust me, it'll be fun."

43

I fold my arms. "Last time I checked, fun didn't include falling on your head."

"I'm not gonna drop you, Cupcake." He glares at me incredulously. "I lift two of you before breakfast." I shake out my arms to expel the nerves. *He's only a few yards away, and the fall probably wouldn't hurt too bad.* "I'm not gonna drop you!" he repeats with a laugh, practically reading my mind.

"Ugh, fine," I huff, unable to back down. I dig my blades in the ice and push off, skating towards him, careful not to go too fast in case he does, in fact, drop me.

The slower I go, the less it'll hurt.

I bend my knees on approach, ready to jump and—*I'm gonna break my neck*—slam directly into Porter's chest, taking him with me to the ice. We slide across the cool surface, his arms holding my waist as we come to a stop.

"Damn," Porter groans. "I said jump into my arms, not tackle me like you're at football tryouts."

I leave my face buried in his chest to allow myself a breath of relief we're both not dead. And maybe also to hide some of the embarrassment as a chill sets into my bones so close to the ice. My adrenaline is so high I can almost ignore the fact I'm lying directly on top of one of the finest men I've ever met.

Glancing up, our eyes connect, and I fight a smile, setting my chin on his chest. "Did I make the team?"

"That depends. Are you alright?" he asks.

"Yes, but my ego may be bruised," I say with a cheeky grin.

"I told you to trust me," he says, brushing a strand of hair out of my face. "This only works if you trust me."

I clear my throat, pushing off him. "Alright. Then let's try again."

"What?" he scoffs, standing to join me.

"Mama didn't raise no quitter," I say, skating back to my starting position. "Let's do this."

I spin to face him, and he's staring at me with an expression I can't quite decipher. He looks... happy? Not a Porter face I'm familiar with.

"Okay," he says, preparing for take two. "Hit me."

8
PORTER

KNOX

Are you in for tonight?

ME

I already told you four times I'd be there.

KNOX

Okay well I wasn't sure if you got tied up in another cheerleader related incident

ME

...

KNOX

I knew it. Why didn't you call me?

ME

You told me not to bother unless the story got better

Spoiler alert - it hasn't

KNOX

Yet

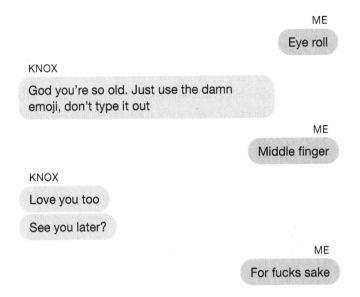

ME

Eye roll

KNOX

God you're so old. Just use the damn emoji, don't type it out

ME

Middle finger

KNOX

Love you too

See you later?

ME

For fucks sake

"God, I need a hot bath," Andi groans while removing the skates, and an image pops in my mind of her lying naked in my tub, bubbles surrounding her body as she—"You know, I think your mom was right."

I shake away the intrusive thought. "I'm sorry, I don't recall you ever having a conversation with my mother."

"I didn't," she says, staring at me like *I'm* the one talking nonsense. "You told your mom at the airport you were gonna try to have some *actual* fun."

"Oh," I reply. *She was listening?* "Didn't realize you were eavesdropping on my private conversation."

"Well, it became no longer private when you sat down directly next to me," she replies, smiling sweetly. "So anyway, she was right. You need to loosen up a little. Go with the flow. Release some tension. Get out of your head."

"And how do you suggest I do that?" I ask, sliding on my tennis shoes.

"You could help me with the rest of the list?"

My lips part as I struggle to look away from her hopeful face. "I don't know if that's such a good idea," I finally answer.

"Come on, Coach," she pleads, placing a hand on my forearm. I hear it daily, but it gives me a rush coming from Andi's mouth. Like she's reminding me I'm in charge. "Christmas is days away, and you don't even have a damn holiday candle at your place."

"I didn't intend to be here for Christmas."

"Well, *news flash,* old man, you are. And it seems you could use a little holiday cheering up," she says, and I narrow my eyes, contemplating her. "Stella, my opponent, already has Theo Schroeder helping her, and you and I both know that's a totally unfair advantage."

Schroeder is one of my most competitive players, but as hard as he works on the field, he's a bit of a party boy off it. I'll let it slide so long as it doesn't affect my team. "Well, if she's got Schroeder, then you're definitely gonna need a hand." *Or two...*

"School's out. I'm not your student. And I'm not asking you to sell a kidney or screw me six ways to Sunday." *Ignoring that tempting suggestion...* "I can figure those checklist items out somehow. But come on. You're the one who reminded me Mama didn't raise no quitter. I didn't peg *you* as one, plus we already started this thing together."

"But you're..." *My ex's little sister.* "I just..." *Can't stop thinking about you naked.*

"Is this about Jess?" she asks.

"I mean, not entirely but—"

"In case you haven't figured it out yet, Jess. Isn't. Here. She's in Virginia, wrapping presents and singing Christmas carols with her *husband.* So if you think you're doing her some big favor by avoiding me, I can assure you she doesn't give a shit who I spend my time with."

"Wow, harsh, Cupcake."

"Harsh. Blunt. Honest. Whatever you wanna call it, it is what it is."

Don't see the holiday festivities as distractions, but rather a break that will allow you to come back refreshed with a new perspective. Maybe this is exactly what I need.

"Come on, please don't make me do it alone," she pouts, with big brown puppy dog eyes. "That's no fun."

"Fine." The word is out of my mouth before I can stop it. I know I'm going to regret this, but I can't help but be at least a little tempted by the idea of spending the holidays with little Ms. Mischief and her list.

"Yes!" She cheers, clapping her hands together. "Okay, that was easier than I thought it'd be."

"Lucky for you, I have some free time," I reply, trying to maintain my persona of nonchalance. "But I do have a question. You know, before I sign on the dotted line and all that. The bottom said 'get naked at Desert Bowl'?" *I really hope it doesn't mean what I think it does, because there's no way I can allow it.*

"I'm telling you this as a mischief maker and *not* the CBU head coach, okay?"

"Okay," I confirm hesitantly.

"The loser has to streak after the bowl game in Arizona." All the blood rushes south at the thought of her running naked. "Porter?" She snaps in front of my face. "Did I break you with the mention of nudity?"

"Have you lost your mind?" I ask in disbelief after

49

coming back to reality. "Streaking at a football game is illegal. You would go to *jail*. And while I—"

"Calm down," Andi says, putting her hands up. "You're gonna give yourself a damn heart attack."

"Calm down?" I scoff. "That's abso—"

"I can assure you we are *not* planning on streaking through the field in front of all those people. Do I look insane to you?"

"Well, no, but—"

"We're going to streak outside our *hotel*, after the game."

"That's still probably illegal and definitely against school policy," I remind her.

"Come on, Mr. Buzzkill, be a good sport."

"You're not worried about being seen?" I ask.

"Not really." She shrugs. "We'll do it late at night when no one should really be out."

"Sounds like you at least partially thought it through," I say, grabbing my bag.

"We have."

"Fine, but if those are the stakes, we better make sure you win."

"Yes, good attitude." She pats me on the shoulder, and we make our way toward the exit. "Any other questions?"

I mull over the list in my mind. "Yeah, what's the triple gumdrop?"

Andi stops dead, and I turn to face her. She stares up at me with big doe eyes and a mischievous smile on her face that screams trouble. It also screams *bend me over and fuck me sense-less*, but I'm gonna pretend my brain didn't translate it properly.

"Again, let's have a rule that for the next week, anything I tell you is as Porter, my fellow mischief maker, and not a buzzkill faculty member."

"If you keep calling me that, we might not have a deal."

I'm glad the perfectly curated reputation I portray at CBU has made an impression, but in my personal life, no one would consider me a buzzkill. I just like to have my fun in private.

"Do you wanna know what it is or not?" she asks with a knowing smirk.

"Fine. Tell me."

Her chestnut eyes hold mine as she confidently says, "It's a threesome."

"A what?" I ask stupidly.

"Well, when three people like each other very much—"

"I know what a threesome is," I retort as we continue walking.

"You sure? Cuz I can draw a diagram if you'd—"

"That won't be necessary." I glare at her.

"Yeah, so *obviously* you can't help with that one, but I'll figure something out."

What the hell does she even mean?

"So are you just gonna go to the bar with a sign saying 'Hump me. I'm horny, wanna have a threesome?'"

"I'd like to think I have a *little* more game than that, Coach." She grins, patting me on the chest.

"Let me see the list again," I say, holding out my hand. She sets it in my palm, and I unfold it before taking a picture with my phone. "I think we can mark off one of these tonight."

"Yeah? Which one?" she asks as I hold the door open for

her to exit the building. I follow her into the sunshine, and we stop on the sidewalk.

"It's a surprise. I'll pick you up at five." Bending down, I brush my lips against the shell of her ear and whisper, "Wear something festive."

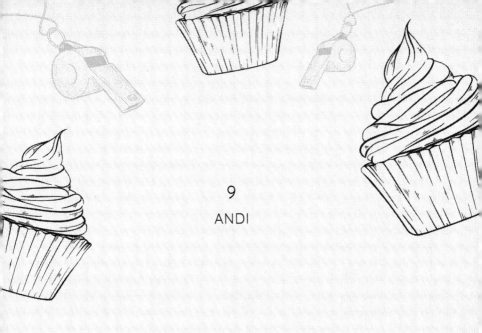

9

ANDI

"Oh, come on," I beg. "Can't you at least tell me what we'll be tackling?"

"Nope," Porter says, hands gripping the steering wheel with that sexy confidence I hate. At a red light, his eyes flick to me briefly, and I can't help but wonder if he's appraising the skimpy elf costume I chose at his instructions to wear something festive.

"Not even a hint?" When he doesn't play along, I opt to fuck with him instead. "Never mind. I know what it is."

He raises a brow. "Oh yeah? And what would that be?"

"The triple gumdrop. For sure." I note the way his jaw ticks as he readjusts his grip. "You seemed eagerly curious about that one."

"Cute," he grits out.

"Cute? Okay, maybe we're not thinking about the same thing. See, in my version, partner number one is bent over, spread open and—"

Porter lifts a hand to stop me. "Thank you, I think I can grasp the concept just fine without your visual aid."

"Suit yourself. It's an excellent visual aid. Got me through quite a few lonely nights."

"Another unnecessary visual aid," he grumbles under his breath.

"What'd you say?"

"Nothing." He clears his throat. "I saw you had gingerbread man tower crossed off. What's up with that?"

"It wasn't very gender inclusive."

"Noted," he replies casually. "So your plan is a triple girl gumdrop?"

I choke on a laugh. "Wow, look who's coming out of his swamp."

"Well, if we're going to be doing this holiday-hell-with-it list, I'm gonna have to stop being Mr. Buzzkill, right?"

"It's the Merry Mischief List, actually. And I don't really have a plan for that yet. It's more of a hope-the-gumdrops-fall-in-my-lap type of situation considering every person I'd consider asking is out of town." He nods, turning into the parking lot of a church. "I'm sorry, was I too unholy? Gotta take me to confession before we can continue our planned activity?"

"This *is* the planned activity," he says with a smirk, pulling into a spot.

"Never would've seen you as the church-on-a-Tuesday kinda guy."

"I'm more of the holiday-festival-at-a-church kinda guy," he says, cutting the engine and getting out of the car.

I follow his lead, and we're surrounded by tons of kids and parents eagerly heading towards the festivities. A mother with an updo so tight it's permanently stretched her face glances my way, and her eyes roam my body in disapproval. I glance down at the decently revealing elf costume I wore thanks to Porter's directions.

Your kids have seen more at the beach, Mother Teresa.

Porter comes to my side of the car, eyes dropping down my body in… amusement? Enjoyment?

"Ready to go?" he asks.

"Really?" I scoff. "Mr. Buzzkill has nothing to say about me rolling up to a church festival looking like a holiday hooker?"

He shrugs. "I said wear something festive. You are. Glad to know you can follow directions."

"Mm-hmm."

"I mean, I thought you'd wear an ugly Christmas sweater or something," he says, eyes roaming me over from head to toe. "But this is good too."

I ignore the way his gaze lights every exposed part of my body on fire and sputter, "We live in Florida. It's ninety-five degrees out. Why the hell would I wear a sweater?"

"Or T-shirt," he says, gesturing down to his shirt, which has the picture of a snowman made of footballs with a Santa hat on top.

I cock my head with a grin. "Cute."

"I was hoping you'd think so." He pulls something out of his back pocket and tosses it at me. It's a shirt identical to his, just smaller.

"Wow. I'm impressed," I say, holding the T-shirt. "You really brought a backup in case my outfit choice didn't make the cut?"

"I like to be prepared for the worst-case scenario."

"Is forgetting really grounds to be considered a worst-case scenario?" I say, tugging the shirt over my head. "Or would it be me showing up to Jesus's house in a stripper outfit?"

"I think there are *many* people who would not consider you in a little elf outfit a worst-case scenario," he says as we walk towards the church.

"Does that list of people include a workaholic football coach with a habit of injuring people?" I ask teasingly, hoping he'll open up a bit more and stop seeing me as a student or Jess's kid sister and just... me.

His eyes hold mine. "You're gonna be trouble, aren't you?"

"Is that a problem for you?" I ask, hooking my arm through his.

"To be determined," he replies as we arrive at the outdoor festival where colored lights are strung all about. There's a variety of food stands, a massive blown-up snowman, a manger scene complete with a real baby Jesus who's currently crying his ass off, and tons of games and activities for the kids.

"How'd you know about this event?" I ask, taking in the merry scene.

"The church runs an athletic charity for underprivileged kids in the community. I volunteer here sometimes."

"Wow." I give his arm a brief squeeze. "The ogre does have layers."

"Just like an onion." Porter winks as we stop at a stand manned by a guy with his broad-shouldered back to us. He turns around, and I recognize him immediately.

Kensington Knox, #52, defensive cornerback for the Tampa Barracudas.

I may be a cheerleader, but I grew up in a football household. Dad's been a diehard Barracudas fan for as long as I can remember. We even had season tickets growing up and went to every game. Probably why it's not a shock I became a cheerleader and major in sports medicine.

"Finally!" Kensington says, grabbing Porter's shoulder and pulling him in for a hug like they're old friends. Then again, Porter did play for Tampa once upon a time, so it wouldn't be a stretch.

"I told you I'd be here," Porter replies with an eye roll.

"Well, I'm glad you could make it with your..." Kensington gives me a brief once-over. "Busy schedule."

My eyes bounce between them, sensing there's more at play than just football.

Kensington extends his hand towards me. "You must be Pop Tart?"

I glare at Porter before returning my attention to Kensington and sliding my hand in his. "Cupcake, actually. But my friends call me Andi."

"Well, nice to meet you, Andi." He grins, giving my hand a soft squeeze before pulling back. "Mine call me Knox."

"You told him about me?" I ask Porter, trying to hide the surprise in my tone.

Knox replies for him, "You'll learn quick enough, he tells me everything."

"Good to know," I mumble.

"Alright, well, I gotta make the rounds," Knox says. "Have fun. We'll catch up later, yeah?"

"Yeah, see you," Porter says, and Knox whispers something in his ear, laughing before waving at me and walking off.

"So *that's* how you ended up volunteering here, huh? Your *bestie,* Kensington Knox?"

Porter grins at me with narrowed eyes. "I figured you knew who he was."

"Of course I do," I scoff. "I grew up in a Florida football household. You really think I wouldn't know who the Tampa first line is?"

"You've got some heart eyes," Porter teases.

"Maybe I should ask him to sign my tits." I puff out my chest, and Porter releases a warm laugh.

"I'm sure he'd happily oblige," he says as we walk past the decorated booths. He pauses at a drink stand and buys us each a cup of something.

"Yum," I hum, taking the warm drink. "Hot chocolate?" He guides us away, behind an inflatable Santa, and pulls something out of his pocket. A laugh rips out of me as I stare down at two mini Baileys bottles being held in his large hand.

"*Spiked* hot chocolate," he says with a grin.

"You smuggled booze for your slutty elf into a *church*?"

"Even Jesus drank wine," he says, twisting off the tops and spiking each of our drinks.

"You really aren't what I expected."

He tips the cocoa towards me, paired with a mischievous grin. "To unwrapping new surprises."

"To unwrapping new surprises."

"Okay, I never knew playing reindeer ring toss could be *so* hard," I say, walking away from the beer bottles decorated like Rudolph. We spent half an hour and forty dollars trying to hook tiny rings on them without avail.

"I think it's one of those things, the drunker you are the better you get," Porter says with a pointed look.

"Yeah, well, I guess one spiked hot chocolate does not a reindeer ring toss champion make."

"What about *two* spiked hot chocolates?" Porter says slyly, showing me a few more baby bottles of Baileys in his pocket.

"Damn, you got a whole factory in those pants or what?"

He waves a hand at his body. "Preparation is part of my assured success routine."

"Whatever strokes your north pole," I reply, patting his shoulder.

We grab two more hot chocolates, each going down smoother than the last, and I find myself enjoying Porter's company more than I expected.

"Ready for a reindeer ring toss rematch?" I ask.

"I actually had something else in mind," he says with a sly smile.

"Care to share with the class?"

"Nope." His eyes fall to my feet, then wander slowly back to mine. "You just wait here and count to a hundred."

"What? Where are you—"

"Patience, Cupcake. I'll be right back," he says before disappearing into the small crowd. My phone buzzes, and I pull it out to a photo of a giant snowman wearing a bikini top.

STELLA
Checked off the big balls. That's four for me

ME
Which four?

STELLA
Guess you'll find out after Christmas

ME
Lame

STELLA
Your tally?

ME
Two...

STELLA
One of those better be 'Block Olivia'

ME
Gotta go, love you

STELLA
Yeah yeah... go blow Santa

Actually, don't. That's too easy a point for you and your lack of gag reflex

ME
Don't hate the player, hate the pecker

A cold, wet thump against my head pulls my attention from the screen.

"What the..." I look up just in time to see another projectile heading straight for me. I throw my arm in front of my face and block a... what? Porter stands a few yards away, tossing a snowball up and down in the palm of his hand as the cold ice soaks into my skin.

"Where did you even get these?" I ask with a laugh as a young kid runs up and sets down a bucket of snowballs next to me.

"Snow cone machine," he says, gesturing with his head toward the stand mass producing buckets of snowballs.

"This is amazing."

Another cold projectile hits the back of my head, and I spin around to find a grinning Knox with his own bucket.

"I'd pretend I was targeting someone else, but my aim is pretty flawless," he says with a cocky grin.

"You're a defender. I wouldn't be surprised if your aim was shit," I quip, and he throws another one, hitting me right in the tits.

"Hey!" I protest, reaching down into my bucket.

"I grew up playing baseball too, gorgeous," Knox says, beaming. "Never underestimate your opponent."

"Alright, you two," Porter shouts, pulling my attention to the most breathtaking, carefree smile I've seen from him yet. He and Knox share a look, and I grab my bucket, stumbling backwards towards a big open area of the outdoor festival.

"This is totally unfair!" I protest.

Porter ignores me entirely. "Three... two... one... Fire!"

Snowballs dart across the open space, and I crouch to grab some from the bucket they supplied me with. I'm pelted left and right, my clothes getting soaked in the process.

"Come on, Knox," I shout out, throwing my own ammunition. "Join the dark side."

"I thought you'd never ask!" he calls back immediately, turning his aim for Porter.

"Traitor!" Porter shouts, shielding himself from both of us as we absolutely demolish him.

"I'm out," Knox calls out, running to shield me. He turns his back and takes the brunt of Porter's "ammo" as I reach in the bucket and pull out the last few snowballs.

"Thanks for the block," I say, looking up at his stupidly perfect face.

"Anytime." He winks, and if I wasn't soaked before, I am now. "Make those count."

He spins out of the way, and Porter and I hold eye contact, each ducking the other's shots while inching closer to one another.

A single snowball remains in his hand, and I beam at the two in mine. "You only got one shot. Don't blow it."

He takes another stride closer, and a snowball hits him directly in the face.

"Guess I found one more," Knox says, releasing a deep laugh. I take the distracted opportunity to blast Porter two more times directly in the chest.

"Hah!" I shout.

Porter bolts for me, and I spin to get away. He scoops me into his damp, muscular arms, lips finding my ear and whispers, "I play to win, Andi. If I ever blow it, it'll be on purpose." He busts the snowball against my neck and steps away, leaving me freezing and flustered.

"You good, Pop Tart?" Knox asks with a knowing grin, and I roll my eyes at him.

Porter heads to the snowball stand and hands over a wad of cash with a big smile. "Keep 'em coming."

He grabs our buckets, and as he hands them to Knox and me, there are a few things I'm absolutely certain of.

Porter is not the Mr. Buzzkill I thought he was.

He and Knox are a tempting blend of sugar and spice.

Throw in my zest, and we've got the perfect recipe for some gumdrop mischief.

"Now you can mark *two* more items off your list," Porter says as we get into his SUV.

I think about Stella's text earlier. One swipe of my finger, and we'd be tied.

"Hold on," I say, pulling out my phone to find Olivia's contact. She's clearly moved on, and there's no reason to keep receiving her hate texts. My knee bounces anxiously, and I do what should've been done days ago. "Make that three. I blocked Olivia."

"Really?" he asks, his tone more pleased than expected.

"Yeah." I glance up, eyes connecting with his. "Really."

"Attagirl." He reaches out, placing a hand on my bare knee, and I still on contact. "I'm proud of you."

"For what?" I ask, surprised by how his touch warms me. "I'd think someone your age would think blocking is childish."

"Why?" He pulls his hand back. "It's never childish to remove yourself from someone, or something, that doesn't serve you."

"I guess." The air conditioning blasts on us, and in the wet T-shirt, I'm bordering on hypothermia. I tug it off, and as the air hits my damp skin, I realize it would take being naked to not have sopping wet clothing on. A shiver shakes through me, and Porter reaches behind his seat, then tosses something in my lap. I hold up the black T-shirt with a white Batman logo on it.

"In case you wanna change into something dry," he suggests, clearing his throat and turning away to give me privacy. I peel off the wet elf top—*the girls are frozen; I'm ditching the bra too*—and slip on the dry T-shirt.

"Much better," I moan, sinking into the seat. "Thank you."

"Welcome," he says, returning his gaze to mine. His eyes drop slowly to my mouth, and I fight away the illusion he could be thinking about kissing me.

He'll never see you as more than Jess's kid sister.

The drive home is quiet, and we say a quick goodbye after he drops me off at my building.

A smile is plastered on my face as I make my way upstairs. It never leaves even as I strip off my clothes to shower before bed. Especially not when I take an extra whiff of Porter's T-shirt before tossing it on the counter. I twist the knob of the shower, and it sputters before shutting off. "What the hell?"

Please be a "me" problem. Rushing to the sink, I twist the handles and… nothing. "Are you kidding me?"

A quick call to building maintenance confirms my fears: the water's out on my floor, and they can't fix it until *after* Christmas.

Happy fucking holidays.

10

PORTER

"Listen," Andi says, readjusting the strap of a beach bag over her shoulder. "This is one of those 'trust the process' things."

"Easier said than done, isn't it, ice princess?" I reply, lugging the shovels and buckets towards the beach.

"Could you just…" She raises her brows at me. "Okay?"

"Fine," I concede. "In Andi I trust."

"Thank you." She beams as we trudge through the warm sand and settle a few yards from the shoreline.

"So are you and Stella sharing score cards, or is this like a 'we'll see who won when we're done' type of situation?"

"Right now, it's four to four," she says, competitive spirit peeking through. "But after today, we should have two more, easy."

After we've arranged our towels, Andi grabs the hem of her oversized Guns N' Roses T-shirt and tugs it upwards. I try *and fail* not to let my eyes drink in every drop of her body as she pulls it off and tosses it in her bag. Her little blue bikini accentuates her curves, and my eyes are drawn to her thick thighs. Crystal Bay cheerleaders aren't only trained to dance and do a high kick. They're true gymnasts. True *athletes.* Which is abundantly clear with every definition of muscle on Andi's body.

"Do you even know who Guns N' Roses is?" I tease to stop my ogling.

"Really?" Andi says, rubbing a bit of sunscreen into her shoulders, making it harder to look away. "I grew up on NFL and '80s rock music. Don't insult me."

"You grew up on Justin Bieber and the Jonas Brothers."

"And? Why limit yourself? I like to dip my toes in all types of water," she replies, reaching down to rub lotion onto one of her long legs. *I wonder if they feel as soft as they look.*

"Mm-hmm," I hum, struggling to look away as she switches legs.

"What's wrong, Coach? Not used to seeing a girl apply proper sun protection?"

My eyes meet hers. "I think I can handle seeing a beautiful woman in a bathing suit."

"Beautiful, huh?" She steps away and shoots me a mischievous smile. I clench my jaw, cursing myself for letting the compliment slip. "Thanks again for last night," she says, tone softening from playful to friendly.

"Of course. I had a good time," I admit because it's the truth. It was the most actual fun I've had in months. My routine, while great for winning games and succeeding in my career, doesn't leave much room for it. I try to get out once or twice a month to blow off a little steam. Okay, to be honest, Knox *forces* me out, but even still, I could probably use more of it.

My eyes swing to Andi bending down to get something

out of her bag, and I curse the little voice in my head reminding me she's a bad idea. It doesn't matter if she's beautiful or funny or has the confidence of a Super Bowl winning quarterback. I can never have her.

"Alright, Porter," Andi says, pulling me out of my personal TED Talk. She's wiggling two sand buckets and small shovels at me. "Time to build some snowmen."

"Snow?" *Just trust the process, Porter, and stop questioning everything.*

"Sandmen, whatever." She waves me off. "Obviously a true snowman is out, so I figured it's the actual *shape* of the snowman that matters. We're gonna make the fattest, roundest sand snowman ever created. And then I'm gonna be one check mark closer to beating Stella."

"Alright." I grab the shovel and a bucket. "Let's make some snow babies."

After one hour and three hundred buckets of sand, we're finally done.

"What do you think?" Andi asks, posing proudly next to her life-size sandman complete with a mangrove seed nose, seashell button eyes, and matching mouth.

"I think that's the best sand snowman you could make in these conditions."

"In these conditions?" she scoffs. "This is the best there could *ever* be. A sandman masterpiece, if I say so myself." She pats the back of the "snowman," and the head tumbles off, splatting against the ground. "Shit."

"Nobody has to know," I say, bending down and molding what's left of the head with some water we had in a pail and plop it back on.

"Who's gonna know?" She shrugs casually.

"*No one's* gonna know," I repeat.

We tilt our heads staring at the now deformed "snowman."

"It said I had to make one. Didn't say it had to live." Her eyes glide to mine. "I'm counting it."

"Oh, definitely." I nudge her shoulder with mine. "A win is a win."

"A win *is* a win," she responds. "Okay, next item on the list!"

"We just spent an hour making Frankensnow. No breaks?"

"No rest for the wicked," she says, grabbing my arm and tugging me to a dry spot away from the shoreline. She settles in the sand, lying flat on her back, and throws out her arms and legs in a starfish position.

"What are you..." A childlike joy settles in me as I watch her make sand angels without a care in the world. *Damn, is she hot.* She jumps up, sand trickling off her body, and beams at her work.

"Looking good," I say, staring down at the sand angel.

"Yeah, but she's lonely." Andi pouts, turning to face me. "Don't let her be lonely, Porter. I know you're not a monster."

"I thought I was an ogre."

"They don't like to be alone either."

"That's literally the entire point of *Shrek*. He *wants* to be alone."

"Did you even *watch* the movie? He only *thinks* he wants to be alone." She gestures towards her creation. "In reality, he's happier with his princess and donkey."

"Guess there's nothing wrong with a little ass." I get down in the sand and add another.

"Attaboy," Andi praises, and I stand up, smiling at our angels side by side.

"There, another item complete."

"Sweet! Six to four, baby!" she cheers, slamming her body into me with a full force chest bump. The gesture catches me off guard. *You can definitely tell she's surrounded by football players.*

I brush some sand off my chest, and she glances down, bringing a hand to her own. She wipes at it furiously but barely any is removed. "This stuff is stuck like glue," she says as her breasts bounce around like coconuts in a hammock.

"Wanna hit the showers before we leave?" I suggest, darting my eyes away.

"Yeah, sounds good."

We gather our things and head to the outdoor showers near the parking lot. Only one is open, and I gesture for her to go first. She steps under the shower head, and it's difficult to drag my eyes away as the water streams down her body and between the valley of her breasts.

Pull yourself together, Porter.

I force my eyes away, pretending to focus on the people passing by. Two women in tiny bikinis smile and wave at me, and now I feel like an even bigger creep.

"Man, that was a good call," Andi says, grabbing a towel and wrapping it around her. "At least now I won't have to sleep with sand up my ass."

"What do you mean?" I ask, trying to avoid the visual.

"The plumbing is out at my place, so that was the closest I'll get to a legit shower."

"What do you mean?" I repeat like an idiot.

Her annoyed eyes shoot to mine. "It means I used to have running water, and now I don't."

How can a person survive without access to water? "When will it be fixed?"

"Well, on account of Christmas, probably a few days after if we're lucky," she says as I take my turn to rinse off.

"So how have you been using the bathroom?" I ask as the cool water runs down my body.

"I dug a hole behind my building," she says, and I stare at her in disbelief. "What the hell do you think? It just went out last night, and you picked me up this morning."

"So you... held it?"

"Oh, good god. Do I need to spell it out for you, Porter? Are you that concerned about my bathroom usage?"

"Sorry," I say with a laugh, running my hands through my wet hair. "It's the first thing I thought of."

"Of course, because you're Mr. Practicality."

"Well, you can use the shower at my place," I suggest, shutting off the water and grabbing my towel.

"I didn't mind doing it here."

"You didn't even use soap," I point out. "And do you know how unsanitary it is to wash off where hundreds of other people do daily?"

A shiver runs down my spine as I think about where I just stood.

"You're a football coach and retired NFL player," Andi scoffs. "You've shared plenty of gym showers with sweaty ass athletes, but you draw the line here?"

"Just because I did it doesn't mean it was my preference. And besides, I intend on *actually* showering when I get home. This was only to get the sand off so I don't have to vacuum every square inch of my car. We can stop by your place so you can get clothes before heading to mine."

"Fine, Porter," she says, smiling sarcastically. "If you really want my wet, soapy body in your shower *that* bad, then I surrender."

I clench my jaw, trying to fight off the mental image she supplied. "Stop being a brat and go get in the car."

"Yeah, you were right," Andi says, walking into the living room in sweats and a sports bra with a towel wrapped around her hair. "That was the most glorious shower I have *ever* taken. Who has *two* rain heads?"

"Well, I tho—"

"Oh my god!" she says, plopping down on the couch next to me. "Is it so you can shower with your fuck buddies?"

I smirk. "It's definitely not a *disadvantage...*"

"Genius." She laughs. "You got any food in this place? I'm starving."

"I ordered Chinese." Her face lights up at the news. "It'll be here soon."

"Maybe you're more Prince Charming than Shrek after all. Two pulsating shower heads, Chinese food... What's next? I bet you love giving foot rubs." *Nothing wrong with giving some pretty feet a little attention.* I glance down to her feet, and she gasps. "Oh my god, you do! You have a foot fetish!"

"Fetish is a strong word," I argue. "I just don't have a problem rubbing a pretty girl's feet."

"You totally have a fetish. That bodes well for me." She places her legs on my lap, waggling her manicured toes. "I've made fifteen thousand dollars selling feet pics on Only Fans this year. People say I have nice feet. My tuition fees thank them."

"Fifteen thousand dollars?" I balk, taking one of her feet in my hand and holding it upwards. "For feet pics?"

"Are you one of my subscribers?" she taunts, poking me in the side with her free toe, and I can't help but laugh.

"Sorry to disappoint you, but I am not," I say, placing her leg back in my lap.

"Aww, too bad for you. I've got some great holiday content up." She sits up straight. "Hey, I have an idea! Let me take a picture of you licking my toe, and we can split the compensation."

That should not be such a turn-on.

A heavy sigh escapes me. "Why did I offer you my shower again?"

"Because you're a stickler for proper hygiene," she says, lying back down. "Don't worry. I'm now clean head to *toes*."

"Wonderful."

"Let's watch a Christmas movie," she suggests, grabbing the remote.

"Sure, I have *Batman Returns* recorded."

"I'm sorry, what?" She eyes me with an amused grin.

"Batman?" I repeat. "Aka Bruce Wayne, from the DC franchise."

"I know who Batman is." She glares at me. "What I'm wondering is why you're suggesting it."

"*Batman Returns* is set around the holidays," I explain. "There're Christmas themes throughout the entire movie. It's a classic."

"*Elf* is a classic," she argues.

"I was *ten* when that movie came out. It's hardly a classic."

"And I was just born. *Totally* a classic."

"Stop making me feel old," I groan.

"Sorry, Grandpa. Besides, *Batman Returns* is just an excuse for watching superhero movies during the holidays."

"Are you serious?" I scoff. "Batman and Catwoman have a moment under mistletoe. What's more Christmas than that?"

She stares at me with narrowed eyes. "How about *It's a Wonderful Life, Home Alone, Love Actually?*"

"Come on," I say, rubbing my thumbs against the bottom of her foot. She drops her head back against the couch with a light moan. "I'll give you a foot rub. Make it worth your while."

She rolls her head, eyes finding mine, and the corner of her mouth twitches. "Fine, we'll watch the silly bat movie."

11

ANDI

"This orange chicken is orgasmic," I moan as the delicious taste hits my tongue. "I could eat it every day for the rest of my life."

"Yeah, I'm not even ashamed to admit I order from Dragon Wok like twice a week," Porter says with a satisfied smile.

"I would move to Tampa just to eat this anytime I want."

"How do you think I ended up in the townhouse?" Porter says, waving a hand around. "I looked up 'houses for sale near Dragon Wok,' and this was the best option."

"You know," I say before swallowing a piece of chicken, "that wouldn't even surprise me."

"What's your favorite type of food?"

"Definitely sushi," I say easily. "No contest."

"Yeah? That's for sure in my top five."

"When my friends and I have a lot going on, we'll eat sushi, talk shit, and everything bothering us seems to fade into the distance. Hard to be upset when you're stuffing your face with a shrimp tempura roll."

"Maybe we should toss this and order sushi instead?" Porter suggests, reaching for my plate, and I turn away, shielding it.

"Don't you dare."

A deep laugh pours out of him. "No worries, your orange chicken is safe... for now."

I glance at the clock. 10:23 p.m.

"It's getting kinda late. Would you mind giving me a ride home? Or I can call an Uber if you—"

"There's no way I'm letting you take an Uber all alone at this time of night." The concern in his tone has the corner of my mouth quirking upwards.

"So you'll give me a ride?"

"To your place, with no working water, where you can't even take a proper shit? No chance."

"What do you suggest I do then?" I ask, sure he's gonna suggest some rich man solution like a hotel or something.

"Stay here," he says casually, eating another bite of food.

"Really?"

He shrugs. "Why not?"

I stare at Porter, trying to figure out when he was body snatched and replaced with this totally relaxed, you-can-sleep-at-my-place version. "You only have one bedroom."

"Okay? And I'll sleep on the couch like I did the night you drowned yourself in sangria."

"Oh..." I say, mildly disappointed but not surprised. He has set firm boundaries and made it clear he *doesn't sleep with students*, especially not students related to his ex, but each minute we spend together feels like I'm getting more of the real Porter and not the perfect, routine Coach Porter everyone else at CBU gets. "Are you sure your old man back can handle it?"

He glares at me. "This '*old man*' can handle plenty."

A flush sweeps through my body, and I can't help but be curious about exploring those limits. We throw away the to-go boxes, and I follow Porter up the stairs to his bedroom.

"I changed the sheets earlier," he says as we walk in the room.

"Were you already planning to let me stay over?"

"No, it's Wednesday," he replies. *As if that's supposed to mean something to me.*

"Okay, and Wednesdays are…?"

"Sheet changing day."

"*Ohhh*," I coo, walking around the king-sized bed as he helps me fold down the large duvet. "So you're one of *those?*"

"One of what?"

"Those 'routine is routine is routine' people."

"That's a lot of routines," he teases, tossing a pillow at me.

"Well, I just meant you have a strict routine and don't like to budge from it."

He shrugs. "Guess so."

"So what's Thursday?"

A smile twitches the corner of his lip. "Cardio and grocery shopping."

"Wow. Wild Thursday."

"Wait till you find out what Fridays are for." His eyes drop to the bed. *Yes, please.* "Well, uh, I'll be downstairs if you need anything. You can grab some clothes from my closet to sleep in if needed."

"You're sure you don't mind me stealing your room?" I ask. "I can take the couch."

"Absolutely not," he scoffs. "My mother would drag me by my ears if she heard I was letting a woman sleep on the couch while I slept on my ergonomic mattress."

"Well, remind me to thank her for teaching you such wonderful manners."

He pauses in the door frame and places his hand on the knob, forearm flexing in a droolworthy fashion. "Goodnight, Cupcake."

I allow my eyes to drink him in for a moment longer than I should. "Night, Coach."

He shuts the door behind him, and I don't move as the sound of his footsteps on the stairs echoes through the house. Throwing myself on the bed, I'm engulfed by the scent of fresh cotton and laundry detergent.

As pleasant as it smells, I'd rather be surrounded by his scent.

Somehow James Porter is making his way to the top of my Christmas list. But I've been such a naughty girl this year... *Maybe Santa could be convinced to bring me cock instead of coal.*

Porter stands in front of the stove, preparing what looks like some kind of healthy omelet—considering there's not a lick of greasy bacon in sight. His cotton T-shirt is tight enough I can admire—er, notice every defined shoulder muscle. He places his hands on his lower back and stretches for what feels like too long for a fit, retired professional athlete.

"Doing okay over there, old man?" I ask.

He spins to face me, spatula in hand. "I'm doing fine, young lady." He smirks, and I can't stop my eyes from dropping to his bare feet and wandering up his dark sweatpants all the way back to his warm eyes.

"Young lady?" I hop off the bar stool and walk across the room till we're mere feet apart.

"Yeah." He sets the spatula down and crosses his arms over his chest in the commanding way that drives me crazy. "If you're gonna call me old man, then I'm gonna call you young lady."

"Careful, Coach. You're entering Daddy territory."

His brows furrow. "Did you really just compare me to your dad?"

A light laugh escapes me. "Not *my* dad. I said *daddy* territory. You know, like Daddy Dom?"

"Who is Daddy Dom?"

I press my lips together and contemplate him. Do I really believe this fine ass man doesn't know the difference between a dad and Daddy? Then again, I can't pass up the opportunity to make Porter squirm.

"It means a man who likes to be in charge in the bedroom, and if his girl doesn't follow instructions or acts a little stubborn, he'll *punish* her."

"Oh, really?"

"Yep."

Porter studies me, gaze burning into every inch of my

skin, and turns back to the stove. "Be a good girl and grab us some plates, would you?"

My mouth falls open. "You were totally messing with me!" Here I am trying to make him squirm, and he's soaked my panties with a single phrase.

"Whatever do you mean?" he asks innocently, flipping the omelet.

"You can't tell me you know the proper usage of the term 'good girl' but don't know what a Daddy Dom is."

His whiskey eyes find mine. "I suppose I have picked up a few things in my *old age.*"

After breakfast, we settle in the living room with our cups of coffee.

"So what item should we mark off your list today?" Porter asks, plopping down on the couch beside me. His scent infiltrates my system, and I allow myself only one deep whiff. *Why does he have to smell so damn good?* I pull out the list from my phone case and unfold it, reading through for the items unmarked.

Merry Mischief List

- ☒ Build a snowman
- ☒ Ice skating
- ☒ Snowball Fight
- ☐ Kiss Under Mistletoe
- ☒ Drink spiked hot chocolate
- ☐ Decorate a Christmas tree
- ☐ Triple gumdrop tower
  ~~Gingerbread man (or woman) tower~~
- ☐ Bake gingerbread man cookies (XLGD)
- ☒ Block Olivia
- ☐ Blow Santa
- ☐ Elf lick whipped cream off ~~tits~~
- ☒ Snow angels

Loser gets naked at Desert Bowl

"How about the triple gumdrop?" I ask, and he chokes on his coffee.

"How about something else?" he says, wiping a drip of liquid off his chin.

"*Boooring*," I groan.

"Let's decorate a Christmas tree," he suggests. "I never have."

"What?" I gasp. "How have you never decorated a Christmas tree?"

"My mom always did it growing up." He shrugs, gesturing at his place completely void of holiday decor. "And considering I live alone and typically travel home for Christmas, it always seemed kinda pointless to do one."

"How incredibly sad. I can't believe you've never had the joy of decorating a tree and having tinsel in places it definitely does not belong." Porter studies me without responding. "You okay there?"

"Yeah… just…"

"Thinking about where I had the tinsel?"

He fights a smile. "Something like that."

"How big a tree do we want?" I ask, wandering through a row of pines.

"Usually my brothers and I found the biggest one we could carry back down the mountain," Porter replies.

"Hold up." I grab his arm. "I thought you've never done the tree thing."

"I said I've never *decorated* a tree, not that I've never taken part in the cutting down of one."

"You actually cut them down yourselves?" My mind wanders to him in a flannel button-up, swinging an ax at a tree stump. Sweat dripping down his forehead as he—

"Sure did," he replies, snapping me out of my lumberjack Porter daydream.

We continue walking through the rows, and I flip the tag

over on a large spruce to check the price. Instead, I stare down at the word "Darla." Confused, I check the tag on another tree: Sunny. And another: Olaf.

"Okay, new mission," I say, spinning to Porter, who's already eyeing me with amusement. "Let's look for whatever tree has the funniest or most unique name."

"This is a tree tent in a Walmart parking lot. What names are you expecting to find?" Porter asks.

"I don't know." I wave my arms around. "Humor me."

"Fine, what are the stakes?"

"Loser buys dinner," I say, grinning. *Girl's gotta eat.*

"I feel like I'm being played here since I'm assuming *you* have final say on any tree we choose, but sure, the loser buys dinner."

He grabs my shoulders, spinning me back towards the rows of trees. Considering we're only a few days from Christmas, the options are rather *limited*. We split up to scour through the selection.

Twenty trees down, and nothing more interesting than "Jellybean."

"I've got a Richard," Porter calls from the row over.

"Unless it says Dick in parentheses, I'm not interested!" I call back, flipping a tag. "I've got a Holly. That's festive."

"*Boringggg*," Porter replies.

"Okay." I continue looking through the options, feeling like this may have not been as fun a challenge as I hoped. I make my way towards the front, looking at the tiniest Christmas trees they have. There's one about four feet tall but flush and full.

"What's your name, little guy?" I mutter to myself, checking the tag.

Spruce Wayne.

A wide grin spreads across my face. I have definitely won this. What are the odds I find a freaking Batman Christmas tree while in the company of someone I know is a fan?

"Oh, Porter!" I shout. "I've found our tree."

A minute later he joins me, and I show him the nametag.

"Did you write that on there yourself?" he accuses.

"Excuse me?" I scoff, throwing a hand over my chest. "I am many things, Coach, but I am *not* a cheater."

He nods his head. "Well, good work. Guess you get to keep your Only Feet money." He drops his mouth to my ear. "For now."

A laugh escapes me. "It's called Only Fans."

"My name is better," he says, walking off to buy the tree. I use the moment alone to take a selfie next to our little spruce and send it to Stella.

ME

About to complete the seventh item. Game on, lady!

STELLA

Slacker. I'm at eight

Ugh, what the hell.

Porter carries the tree into his townhouse, and we set it up in the stand. I admire the little spruce, name tag still attached, and think about how fun it's gonna be to—

"Shit," I groan.

"What?" he asks, worried eyes meeting mine.

"We forgot decorations." He ignores me, disappearing down the hallway. "Hello? This is an emergency!"

There's a bit of rustling before he reappears with arms full of shopping bags stuffed to the brim, a shiny silver garland dragging behind him.

"Crisis averted," he says, unable to fight the smug smile on his face.

"What in the *Miracle on 34th Street* is all this?" I say, rushing over to him and grabbing a bag to look through it.

"I may have gotten a little carried away when I went for groceries this morning."

"This morning? I woke up at eight, and you were here making breakfast."

"Okay... and I was up at four," he says, setting boxes of lights on the coffee table.

My face pulls together. "Why would any sane person get up at that ungodly hour?"

He shrugs. "Daddy had things to do."

"Oh god," I groan. "I'm creating a merry monster."

12
PORTER

"She's perfect," Andi says, hands on her hips, staring at our "masterpiece." Twinkling colorful lights and shimmering tinsel she spread like glitter adorn the small tree, ornaments weighing down each branch.

It's hideous and gaudy, but gorgeous all at the same time. We had so many supplies leftover, Andi insisted on decorating the rest of the downstairs, and now it looks like Santa's workshop.

"Great job."

"It was a team effort," she says, plopping down on the couch. "But now I'm exhausted and starving. Can we order from Dragon Wok?"

I check the clock. 11:05 p.m.

"They closed half an hour ago."

"What?" she groans. "That's the worst news I've heard all day."

"Well, lucky for you, I'm buying dinner," I say, grabbing my keys off the counter. "And I know the perfect place."

"To the batmobile!" Andi shouts, almost startling me.

"I think *I've* created a monster."

A bell above the door chimes as we walk into the small diner. This place is about as close to the North Pole as we can get in Tampa.

"What in the holy holiday heaven?" Andi says, looking around at the decorations floor to ceiling. "*You,* the coach who avoids Christmas, comes *here?*"

"Just because I don't decorate doesn't mean I'm anti-Christmas."

"I suppose so." Her eyes sparkle, taking in the scene, and I know I've made the right choice. "Guess you get your fill from this Santa sanctuary."

"They go all out for every holiday," I tell her.

"*Every* holiday?"

"Yep. You should've seen the display they had for President's Day. The servers dressed up with wigs and all. It was spectacular." A deep laugh escapes me as I stop us at an open booth. We sit across from each other, and within seconds, my favorite waitress places menus in front of us.

"James," she says, smiling down at me. "I thought you were gonna be gone the whole holiday."

"Hi, Paula." I smile up at her. "Change of plans."

Her eyes flick to Andi before returning to mine. "Real pretty change of plans."

"If only I could accept the credit," Andi says. "I'm just the *consolation* to the change of plans. Someone had to get this guy out of his boring bachelor pad and into the holiday spirit."

"Something tells me you're no one's consolation prize," Paula replies, and Andi grins bashfully. Paula winks at me before taking our drink order and leaving us to ourselves.

Andi slaps her menu down on the table and grins at me. "Are you into age gap romances?"

"Care to be more specific, young lady?"

"I think Paula has the hots for you, Coach."

I roll my lips together to fight a smile. "That so?"

"Mm-hmm." She brushes a strand of hair off her shoulder, and my eyes drop to her exposed collarbone. My brain screams at me to stop examining the way her throat bobs as she swallows. Instead, they wander to the column of her neck, and I consider what it would feel like under my tongue. Marking her pretty skin up before I venture to places I haven't yet seen.

"So are you?" she asks, pulling my attention back to her eyes.

"Am I what?" My brain is mush. This girl is turning me into an idiot.

"Into age gap romances?"

It seems I could be convinced.

"Paula's not really my type," I say with a cocked brow. "And her husband of forty years might have something to say about me making the moves on his wife."

Andi tilts her head with a teasing pout. "Guess you'll never know what it's like makin' love to a cougar."

"How will I ever survive?"

Paula sets our drinks in front of us and takes our order.

"So how'd you end up at CBU?" Andi asks once she leaves.

"After my accident, the doctors wouldn't clear me to play professionally again. I can still exercise and have total mobility, but they weren't really willing to risk me getting sacked by three-hundred-pound linemen on a daily basis. Since I was a CBU alumnus, I had helped the team out whenever I had time, even when playing for Tampa. Once I was healed and cleared to work, I started as an assistant coach there. Then a few years ago, the old head coach left, and they gave me a shot."

"Do you like it?"

"Yeah, it isn't what I expected for my life. But it gives me purpose, and to be honest, I've never felt better than I do when I'm on the field with those guys, watching them give their all. And the pride I feel when we win and knowing I was a part of that. I found myself again, but it wasn't in the way I thought I would."

"I guess sometimes we find ourselves in unexpected ways," Andi says, toying with her silver necklace, pulling my attention back to that spot I can't stop craving.

"Do you feel like this mischief list is helping you find yourself again?"

"I don't really think I've lost myself, per se. It's just reminding me to focus on the small joys instead of the big fails."

"And Olivia was your big fail?"

"I wouldn't say that." She shakes her head. "I'm perfectly content with the person I am. I like my life and my friends. But every time I date someone it leaves me feeling like I'm not enough. Like I need to change things about myself to fit better in their space."

"You shouldn't shrink yourself down to fit someone else's expectations. And honestly, you really don't seem like the type of woman to do that in the first place."

"Quite insightful for someone who's only really known me a few days."

I shrug. "I've gotten used to reading people over the years. It's kind of required for coaching hormonal, testosterone-fueled football players. Gotta get a read on 'em quick to know the best training method."

"So you're training me to be a better girlfriend?" she teases.

"No, I'm just reiterating what you should already know."

"And what's that?"

My mind swirls, trying to figure out how to explain she should never settle for less. "Okay, so it's like this," I say. "When you go to the store looking for one of those peppermint whatever cupcakes—"

"Peppermint mocha," she corrects.

"Okay, sure. So imagine you go to the store looking for a peppermint *mocha* cupcake, and they only have vanilla."

"A tragedy!" she gasps.

"Exactly." I smirk. "Would you settle for the vanilla?"

"No way," she replies, scrunching her nose. "That would *not* hit the seasonal spot."

"Right, so you'd probably go to another store and keep looking until you found one or a suitable alternative, right?"

"I guess so," she says, narrowing her eyes at me.

"Stop settling for basic relationships that don't fulfill your 'seasonal cravings,'" I say, feeling silly, but the way her face softens lets me know I'm on the right track. "Hold out for that peppermint mocha, or you'll never be fully satisfied."

"Wow," she says with a soft smile. "That's actually some very good, targeted advice. Thanks."

"Anytime."

"Damn, now I want something sweet," Andi says. "They got dessert in this place?"

"Only fifteen different flavors of pie," I say, sliding her the dessert menu just as Paula arrives with our food.

After dinner, Andi demolishes a slice of candy cane pie. When we finally stand to leave, I do a quick stretch to help ease the muscles in my aching back.

"Okay, that's it," Andi says, staring at me unamused. "You are not staying on the sofa again tonight. You clearly can't deal with sleeping on your very attractive albeit utterly uncomfortable couch. I swear modern furniture wasn't made for true functionality—only to look pretty in show rooms and rich guy penthouses." I roll my lips together, fighting the urge to smile because she's a hundred percent right. Her eyes widen, and a laugh spills out. "You *are* one of those rich guys who never uses his couch, aren't you?"

"The girl from the furniture store said it would fit nicely with the rest of the stuff I picked out," I reply.

"Was that before or after you *boned* her?" Andi asks, face full of amusement.

My brows pull together as I wonder how she can read me so well. "After…"

A laugh bursts out of her as we make our way to the exit. "Of course." She pauses a step before the doorway, eyes glued above us. I follow her gaze, landing on a mistletoe hung on the frame.

"Item number eight," Andi says, eyes bouncing around the restaurant.

"What are you looking for?"

"Someone to help me complete the mistletoe challenge."

My eyes drop to her lips as she continues her search.

Is she really looking for someone else?

Then again, I have made it clear I can't because... why? *She's too young? A student? Jess's sister?*

My mind struggles to choose exactly which reason is holding me back. Or if I even give a shit about any of them anymore.

She toys with her necklace, and all my inhibitions exit the diner.

Maybe an innocent kiss is exactly what I need to get her out of my system.

Fuck it.

Taking a step forward, I slide a hand into her hair, cradling her face. My heart pounds as my other hand snakes around her waist, and I pull her with me, directly under the mistletoe.

"What are you—"

My lips cut off her unnecessary question. She's tense for mere seconds before melting to putty in my hands. She tastes like cinnamon and peppermint. Sensual sin and sweet salvation. There's a reason people make candles out of this. It's addicting.

Another quick kiss, and I force myself to pull away.

"There. Item complete. Let's go," I say, gesturing towards the exit, hoping she'll leave before I get the urge to mark the item off twice. She stares at me for a moment, a hand coming up to touch her swollen lips, then turns and walks out of the diner.

For a guy so good at strategizing, I didn't see this blind side coming.

One kiss was supposed to get her out of my system. Instead I've been left with an unsatisfied sweet tooth, craving another taste of cinnamon, peppermint, and *her*.

13
ANDI

The perfectly tucked down comforter taunts us to ruffle its feathers.

Porter kissed me.

Why *did* he kiss me?

Or rather, why did he kiss me like *that?*

His arms around my waist. Lips warm and eager. I would've expected friendly and calculating. Not spontaneous and passionate. *Being wrong never felt so right.*

"I can go to the couch if you're not comfortable with this, truly," Porter says, inching towards the door.

"No," I reply, voice higher pitched than intended. I clear my throat. "No, that's not necessary. Just tired. Lost in thought is all." I throw myself into the bed, belly down. Cool air trickles up my thighs, and I'm reminded all I've got on is an oversized Nickelback T-shirt and boy short underwear. *Oops.*

I wasn't expecting to share a bed when we picked up clothes from my place.

"See?" I say, crawling under the covers and patting the bedspread, gesturing for Porter to join me. "We can be adults about this."

I'd rather act like horny teenagers, but hey, beggars can't be choosers.

"Sure." He lets out a chuckle, sliding into bed wearing nothing but athletic shorts. My eyes hungrily drink in his bare, toned chest, and my fingers ache to trace every ridge. *Of course he sleeps without a shirt on.*

Porter shuts off the main light, leaving us in the dim glow from the bathroom. Only shuffling sheets and soft breaths fill the otherwise still room.

I'm dying to ask about our kiss, but now, lying so close, so intimately, it feels like the absolute wrong time.

Or does that make the timing even more right?

If this silence lasts any longer, I'll end up blurting the question whether I want to or not.

"Thanks again for helping me with the list," I say, fisting the blanket. "And letting me stay here."

"Happy I could help."

Another stretch of silence falls over us. In the low light, my eyes hungrily trace his silhouette, pausing at his waist.

God, it's been a long time since I've had some good dick.

A man as arrogant as him must know how to use it. I wonder if he's as stern in the bedroom as he is on the side-lines. *Will I be punished if I misbehave?*

"What are you thinking about?" Porter asks, interrupting my trip down Coach Pornhub lane.

"What makes you assume I'm not trying to fall asleep?"

"I can practically hear the wheels churning in your brain."

"I was…" *What was I thinking about?* "Thinking about the list and what would be the easiest item to complete next." *Yeah, good save.*

"Don't worry, I've got it covered."

"Is that so?" I laugh, amused at his incessant desire to be in control.

"Yep."

After rolling to face him, I rest my head on my hand. His gaze travels slowly from my toes underneath the blanket back to my eyes, lighting me on fire.

"Must you always be so secretive?" I ask.

"It's more fun this way."

His attention makes me squirm. I'm hyper aware of his proximity as his strong masculine scent surrounds me while I'm tangled in his sheets, his body only inches away. *Come on, Andi. Think of something else to talk about before you kiss this man again.*

"Are you sad you didn't get to go home for Christmas?" I blurt.

"Is it wrong to say no?"

"It's not wrong. Maybe a little Scrooge-like, but not wrong. Why though? You and your family not close?"

"We are. It's not that. I know this is going to sound stupid, but like you pointed out, my routine is everything to me. Without it, I just feel lost," he admits.

"That's not stupid. I get it. I have my pre-game routine too, and I always feel a little off if I don't get to complete it."

"Really?"

"Yeah, I like to eat a light meal. Do some yoga. Listen to a little Lana Del Rey. Really sets the mood for game day."

"Sounds nice," he says, shifting in place. "I guess for me it feels like without it, everything I've worked for would fall apart. Or if I alter my routine by even the smallest degree, it'll shift everything like the butterfly effect and ruin my life."

His admission surprises me. "That's a ton of pressure to put on yourself."

"I know." Silence stretches between us, and I worry he's going to throw back up those steel walls he hides behind. "The last time I veered from the routine, it cost me my career. Feels too risky to let it happen again."

"I don't understand," I say, trying to sort through any information Jess mentioned about the accident, which wasn't much. "I thought you got hurt playing."

Another stretch of silence. "Jess never talked about what happened?"

"No?" A weight settles in my stomach. Was it worse than I knew? Should I have pressed Jess more to talk about it? I thought she was just being private like always. "She and I don't really talk much about personal stuff."

"Sounds like Jess," he says with a humorless laugh.

"Will you tell me about it?"

He releases a soft sigh. "Well, I used to have this pre-game routine, and I never deviated from it. Not since starting college ball and definitely not when I went to the pros. I'd stay home or in the hotel room, spend time alone, no social media or phone calls. No distractions. Just me, a little music, and maybe an audiobook or something to pass the time until we had to be at the stadium."

"Glad some things never change," I tease lightly.

"Yeah, I guess that's true."

"So what happened?"

"One day, before a late afternoon game, Jess asked me to meet her for breakfast. There was a new brunch place downtown and she, I don't know, she said she really wanted to see me, and I was so in love with her I thought, fuck it. One day deviating from the routine shouldn't hurt." I swallow hard, uncomfortable at his admission of his previous feelings for her. "So anyway, we met for breakfast, and then when I was on the way to the stadium, I got T-boned by someone running a red light," he says. "I dislocated my shoulder and broke my back in two places."

"Porter," I gasp. "You agreed to sleep on the couch, and you have a back injury!"

"*Had* a back injury," he corrects. But we both know better. Most back injuries cause long-term damage, which is why he's now coaching instead of playing pro where he should be.

"I know you said you have full mobility, but do you still have tenderness or any other issues?" I ask, physical therapist studies on full display.

"Occasionally, but it's been six years. So I'm fully cleared."

Six years was right around the time—

"Is that why you broke up with Jess?" I blurt.

"I'm sorry?" he scoffs. "*She* left *me*."

"What do you mean, *she left*?" I say, sitting straight up. Jess always made it seem like she was the one who got dumped. Although knowing her, it doesn't surprise me she stretched the truth.

"Well, after it was obvious I wouldn't play in the NFL

anymore, she made a slow exit. I think watching me in recovery was too hard for her. I lost twenty pounds within a month because it was so painful to do anything, including eat. And I looked awful."

"So? You don't leave someone because they're injured. What about 'in sickness and in health?' Shouldn't that apply to the people you're dating too?"

He shrugs. "Not everyone is made to handle that type of situation."

I definitely don't consider Jess weak, but her career is everything to her. And if she felt caring for Porter was a distraction, *that* I can see her abandoning him over. *Even though it's completely fucked up.*

"Do you miss her?" I ask, desperate to know. Our kiss earlier was fireworks, but I can't risk hooking up with someone who's using me to feel closer to my sister. That's plain insulting.

"I miss what we could've been," he says candidly. "The future we planned that we'll never have the chance to have. But her? No, I don't."

I release a quiet sigh of relief. "So that's why you're so stuck on your routine? Because last time you strayed from it, your life blew up? And you're afraid it'll happen again?"

"I guess that about sums it up."

"Seriously?" I scoff. "Porter, that's insane. It was an *accident*. One you could have just as easily had while driving from home to the stadium."

"Yeah, but I wasn't driving from home like I should have been."

"And? It doesn't matter. We're always exactly where we're meant to be. Everything happens for a reason."

"Sometimes things just happen. There's not always a reason."

"I don't know," I say, smiling softly. "I see how the guys look up to you at CBU. You've impacted their lives. You *care* about them. That never would have happened if you hadn't ended up coaching instead of playing pro ball. Maybe you should stop seeing your current life as a consolation prize and appreciate it for what it is."

"And what is it, exactly?"

"The opportunity to make a difference. A *real* difference. And I'm not saying it doesn't suck you can't play pro ever again, because that fucking blows. But you influence the life of every player you coach. They look up to you. Pride themselves on your approval. You have the power to make or break those guys. To bring them up to the caliber of making the pros or weeding out those not suitable for it. Sure, as a pro player you could've scored some touchdowns, won some rich team owner a couple Super Bowls," I tease, trying to lighten the conversation. "But what you're doing at CBU could affect the game of football for years to come. You're training the next generation of pro players. Ball's in your field, Coach. Make it count."

"You give a pretty good pep talk," Porter says, and I lie back down to face him.

"I'm a cheerleader. Pep is in my DNA."

"I guess that is an important qualification."

The room falls quiet once again, and I dislike the idea of us going to sleep after discussing such a sensitive topic. "Alright, enough heavy stuff for the night. What's your favorite Christmas memory?"

"Hmm… that's a hard one," he replies.

"Top of your head. When you think of Christmas, what comes to mind?"

He's quiet for a moment, and just when I think he won't respond, he says, "When I was younger, after my brothers and I would go to bed, or so my parents thought, they'd sneak to the living room to set up our presents. My brothers and I would watch silently from the top of the stairs as they laughed and helped each other put everything together for us. After they were done, my dad would bring in two glasses of red wine, and then he and Mom would slow dance in the living room to 'I Saw Mommy Kissing Santa Claus.'"

"Why does it not surprise me you couldn't even let the magic of Santa exist as a child?"

"The magic was there." He laughs softly. "It just wasn't Santa."

I reach out, placing a hand on his chest. "That's so sweet."

"I guess so," he mumbles, placing his hand over mine and giving it a light squeeze.

"The scrooge has a soft side," I say, and he nudges me under the covers with his foot. I nudge back, and our feet end up entangled.

"What's your most embarrassing Christmas memory?" Porter asks.

"Over my dead body."

"Come on." His foot rubbing against my inner ankle has me struggling to think straight. "I shared; now it's your turn."

"Didn't realize we were playing twenty questions."

"Aren't we?"

I toy with the thin chain around my neck. "Fine, but I

want to preface this by saying I know it was ridiculous, and my family has absolutely never ever let me live it down."

"Don't tempt me with a good time."

"When I was five, I asked Santa for a pink rocking horse, and on Christmas morning, there was this gigantic box in the living room. I was so excited I was shaking. *Finally*, after what felt like an eternity, my parents let me open it."

"Is the embarrassing part coming or...?"

"Just wait," I say, skin flushing with heat at the memory. "So I opened it up, and the rocking horse was fucking *brown.*"

"Brown?" He mock gasps. "Not brown!"

"Yes, brown," I say, hitting him with a pillow. "Like one of those antique wooden rocking horses I'm sure cost them a fortune."

"And that's so bad because...?"

"I was so distraught it wasn't pink, I started bawling right in the middle of the living room with my entire family there."

"That's not even—"

"I got so worked up I barfed on the Christmas tree."

A deep laugh escapes him. "Seriously?"

"Yep, it smelled so bad they had to throw out the tree before we could continue. Jess gives me a barf bag every year before we open presents in case 'I get something in the wrong color.'"

"What had you eaten for breakfast?"

"What kind of question is that?" I ask, considering the truth will just add to the embarrassment.

"Humor me?"

I fight a smile and ultimately cave. "I had a cupcake."

"Only a single cupcake?" He cocks a brow, and I press my lips together.

"Well, a normal amount…"

"How many, Andi?"

There's a long pause in which he rubs his thumb across my wrist, blowing my resolve to pieces. "Fine. It was five."

"Five?" He chokes on a laugh.

"But in my defense, it was Christmas! And Christmas cupcakes don't count."

"I think your family's yakked-on Christmas tree would beg to differ," he says between fits of laughter.

"It went to a perfectly nice junk yard."

"Well, I know what I'm *not* making you for Christmas breakfast," he says. "Wouldn't want to ruin the fine craftsmanship of Spruce Wayne."

"I'm a grown woman who's perfectly capable of eating a few sweet treats without risking the destruction of our beloved tree."

"If you say so, *Cupcake*."

"You're cruel!" I sit up, grab a pillow, and hit him with it repeatedly.

"Oh, now you've done it." He pushes himself up and tackles me to the mattress. His body weight presses down on me, the fluffy pillow all that separates us. "Watch yourself."

"I was only giving you a warning message for teasing me. Did I break your *no bratty vibes* in the bedroom rule or something?"

He drops his head to my ear, tone firm. "Something like that."

I'm not sure if it's his words or his weight that has me blurting, "What are you gonna do about it?"

His warm breath hits my neck, and I allow myself five seconds to relish in the intoxicating distraction of his smell. "Leave you to dream about your pink horses."

He rolls off me, and I already miss the contact.

"It's okay, I—" *Enjoyed it? Wish you'd come back?* "Goodnight." *Goodnight? The fuck was that?*

The sound of shuffling blankets from Porter settling back on his side fills the air between us. "Sweet dreams, Andi."

14
ANDI

"Change of plans," Porter says as I walk down the stairs. "Can't do today's item. Gotta reschedule it."

"Aww, man," I say, pouting. "What was it?"

"Nice try." He turns his back, putting dishes away.

I pull out the list and look down at it. A smirk spreads across my face.

"Guess today's the day I let an elf lick whipped cream off my tits."

"What?" Porter's head whips in my direction.

"Yeah." I shrug. "Seems like an easy enough one."

"Where the hell are you gonna find an elf?"

We walk into Crystal Bay Mall, whipped cream securely stored in my purse, and Porter shakes his head.

"Really?" he asks rhetorically. "A *mall* elf?"

"I'm sorry, do you have a better idea?" His jaw ticks as he looks away from me. "Besides, it's a win-win. Some nerdy guy gets to live out his childhood dream of licking a girl's tits, and I'll be one step closer to crushing Stella."

"Mm-hmm," Porter hums.

We pass through the food court and make our way to Santa's village. The line is easily thirty families deep and backs up all the way to Pizza by the Slice. I groan, stepping behind the last kid, who's explaining his plan to his dad about asking Santa for a Nintendo Switch. He looks to be about eight years old, and he's presenting the reasoning to his father like he's a Harvard-educated lawyer.

"I'll be right back," Porter says before disappearing behind the mock Christmas cottage.

"And honestly, I'm really asking for the entire family," the little boy before me continues. "Think of all the quality family time we'll get together playing Mario Kart!"

I've moved forward about ten kids by the time Porter returns.

"Where'd you go?" I ask, seeing no bags in his hands.

"Bathroom."

"You dig a hole outside? Worked for me."

"Real funny," he says, narrowing his eyes in amusement. "So what's your plan here? You're just gonna go up to Santa and say, 'Can you spare an elf for a moment so he can lick some whipped cream clean off my titties? Please and thank you.'"

A mother in front of us turns around and glares at Porter, covering her kid's ears while her husband steals a glance at my chest.

"No, actually." I smile sweetly. "First, I was gonna ask

Santa if I could borrow *him,* and get one more thing marked off the list."

Porter doesn't need to know I'm bluffing.

He brings his mouth to my ear and whispers, "There's no way I'm letting you blow a goddamn mall Santa."

A welcome shiver runs down my spine. "Why not?"

He glances at the "Santa," whose realistic gray hair and definitely real beard are emphasizing the fact he's at least seventy.

"You know what?" He rolls his lips together. "You wanna blow Grandpa Santa, go right ahead. I won't get in your way."

He steps away and folds those spectacular arms over his perfect chest.

"Good," I clip. "I will."

"Fine. Have fun."

I glance around at all the kids and parents and consider this may not be the best setting for a Christmas hoe-down. After all, at least half of them haven't quite had the chat about what Mommy and Daddy do under the covers at night. "But let's wait until break, and then I'll ask. Doing this with an audience of children may be borderline illegal."

A deep laugh escapes Porter. "Glad you finally figured that out."

We step to the side, and after another twenty minutes, Santa and the elves take their break. I shoot Porter a wink and saunter off, whipped cream in hand. An elf stands to the side with bright red hair and looks to be about twenty. Actually, I better ask his age before I let a fifteen-year-old make a sundae of my tits.

"Excuse me," I say, tapping his shoulder. "How old are you?"

"Nineteen," he says, with a curious smile.

Okay, legal, good to go.

"So I'm doing this winter bucket list thing. And…" I puff out my chest, which is highly visible in the low cut tank top I chose specifically for this endeavor. "One item is to have an elf lick whipped cream off my tits." His mouth parts open, and I wiggle the whipped cream can. "I was wondering if you would like to do the honors."

He glances behind me. "Umm… is your… boyfriend okay with that?"

"He's not my boyfriend," I say, waving Porter off. "Don't worry about him."

"Okay." The elf chuckles nervously.

"So are you down?"

"Is this a joke?" He looks around. "Did my friends put you up to this?"

"What? No. Look…" I shake the can and open it, spraying the whipped cream across my chest. "Are you gonna lick it off or should I find another elf?"

His eyes drop, mouth practically salivating, and he dips down towards my chest. "I'll do it."

A hand grabs my bicep, and I'm tugged away before the elf can get a single taste.

"Damn it, I knew it was too good to be true," I hear him whine as I'm spun around.

"What the hell are you doing?" I shriek as Porter drags me through the mall with his arm around my waist.

He remains silent, pausing by a small alcove and caging me into it.

"Porter," I say, struggling for air. "What's your problem?"

His eyes roam over me, landing on my still whipped-cream-covered breasts.

"I didn't like the way Buddy the Elf was eye fucking you," he says, tone low and gravelly.

"And why would you care?" I ask, holding my breath.

"The kid would've come in his pants if he got even the smallest taste of you. I was protecting the children of the mall from an act of public indecency."

"Bullshit."

He fights a smile. "What can I say? I care about the children."

His eyes don't leave mine for a moment. Our heavy breaths fill the small space as I struggle not to get whipped cream on his perfectly clean T-shirt.

Wait, why do I care?

I break our staring contest and glance down at my chest. "Well, what the hell am I supposed to do about this?"

Porter's gaze follows mine. He places a hand on my neck and tips my head back, gliding his tongue across my skin. I'm shocked speechless as he licks off every last drop. His tongue drags against the column of my throat, and a soft moan slips from my lips.

I'm pretty sure there was no whipped cream there.

A low growl escapes him, and he pulls away, looking down.

"There, all clean. Let's go," Porter says, plucking the whipped cream out of my hand.

He spins and walks away, leaving my mind more tangled than a strand of forgotten Christmas lights.

Where the hell did that come from?

15
PORTER

"So we're not gonna talk about it then?" Andi asks with a huff as we walk into my place.

"What's there to talk about?" I reply, trying not to think about how damn good she tasted. And I don't mean the dessert topping. A single swipe of her neck, and I was tenting in the middle of the damn mall.

Grabbing a rag, I busy myself by wiping down the kitchen countertop, but considering it was Gordan-Ramsay-approved clean when we left, I'm fully aware I look like a psychopath.

"Maybe how you motorboated me in the mall after ruining my chances of marking *two* items off my list?"

I pause, turning to face her. "We both know you weren't going to blow Santa."

She places her hands on her hips. "I might have."

"Sure, when reindeers fly," I mumble, returning to the countertop.

"They do, you idiot!"

"Yeah, in *Rudolph*. As in *fiction*."

"Whatever." She waves me off, obviously flustered. "The elf was a sure thing!"

My jaw ticks at the memory of pimple face's mouth being inches from her chest. "Apparently not," I say smugly, scrubbing at an invisible mark on the counter.

"Oh, good god." Andi snatches the rag away. "This kitchen is spotless. I would eat off the damn floors, so can you please stop avoidance cleaning? You're stressing me out."

"I'm not avoiding." *It's called strategic deflection.*

"Bullshit." She steps closer, invading my space, and my eyes drop to her neck. Just imagining what it would feel like drove me mad before. Now that I know? I'm salivating. "Why did you stop me earlier?"

"I already told you. I was thinking of the children."

"Why did you kiss me last night?" she asks, her expression serious. *Oh, we're really doing this.*

. "Because I... Because you needed to mark it off your list."

"Okay? And you said yourself when we started this there were some things you weren't gonna be helping me with."

"Yeah, well..." I press my lips together, struggling to come up with an excuse.

Because I wanted to.

Because I *craved* it.

Because I've thought about kissing you more in the last week than I've thought about my starting lineup. *Which is definitely not normal for me.*

"Well?" she presses.

"I was helping you out. For the list. It was business."

It was hot as hell.

"Mm-hmm, sure." She crosses her arms, pulling my attention to her perfect chest. The same chest I just had my mouth on. "That brings me back to the elf incident. If you cared *soooo* much about me finishing my list, why'd you stop me?"

"Because of the childr—"

"The *truth*, Porter. Come on." *Fuck, she's hot when she's bossy.*

"I was saving you—"

"Really?" She laughs, stepping towards me, and my hand goes to her hip, struggling to fight the magnetic pull to her body. Our eyes connect, and my pulse beats on overdrive. "So it's not because you wanted his job?"

"Why would—"

"You didn't wish you were the one in the little elf costume about to slurp my tits like the top of a hot chocolate? Weren't imagining everything else you wanted to do to me once we got back here?"

"You're giving my imagination a lot of credit." *Although the hot chocolate analogy is pretty spot on.*

"You aren't fooling me, Porter. Not anymore." Her cognac eyes study me. Strip me down. Make me vulnerable. She's looking straight through me, calling me out on all my bullshit. My gaze falls back to her neck.

That damn neck. Why is it so enticing?

"Stop feeding me ridiculous excuses," she snaps with a glare, all fired up and ready for a fight.

"What do you want me to say?" I ask, stepping forward and backing her toward the kitchen island. "That the idea of that kid getting to taste you, to know what your skin feels like under his lips before I could, drove me fucking mad?" I place my hands on the cool marble countertop, caging her in, and her eyes go wide, lips mere centimeters from mine.

"If it's the truth."

"It doesn't matter if it's the truth," I say, fighting like hell to stay in control. "This can't happen. *We* can't happen."

"Why? Because you dated my sister like half a decade ago?" she asks, embers flickering in her eyes, ready to reignite.

"No." *I stopped caring about that after a single day of knowing you.* "Because in case you forgot, you're a student at the university I *work* for, and if anyone ever found out, my career would be over."

"Why would anyone find out?" she asks. "We're two consenting adults, and I don't go around blabbing about my private life. It's no one's business."

"I know, but shit happens. Sometimes it's out of our control."

"God, you're infuriating!" She huffs, pushing me off and turning away.

"Wait," I say, reaching out and loosely grabbing her wrist.

"What, Porter?" She spins back to face me. "What more is there to say? You keep lying to the both of us, and I'm sick of it. You're so hell bent on staying in control all the time—" A wicked grin spreads across her furious face, making me nervous. "God, I'd love to see you lose it."

I grind my teeth together. "Stop taunting me, Cupcake."

"What are you gonna do?" She juts her lower lip out in a pouty challenge. "Punish me?"

For starters. "You're trouble."

"You have no idea," she says, a finger dragging along the already low hem of her tank top. "Let's play a little game. I'm gonna ask you a question, and every time you lie, I lose a piece of clothing."

"You think I can't handle a little skin? I've already seen you in a bathing suit." *And you looked like a damn angel.*

"We'll see." She contemplates me. "When's the last time you had sex?"

My brows furrow, surprised at her first question. "Three weeks ago?"

"Frequent hook up or one-night stand?"

"One-night stand," I answer honestly.

"Where'd you meet her?"

"Night club."

"And did you get an STD test since then?"

"Of course." I narrow my eyes at her. "The team gets checked once a month, and I'm no exception to that rule."

"Good." She nods. "Now that I've calibrated the lie detector, let's get started."

I huff out a laugh. She's beautifully infuriating. Pushing me around like she's in control. My dick is so hard it's getting painful, and I'm fighting to think straight. I've done so well resisting her, but if she starts stripping in my kitchen... I may be strong, but I'm still human.

"Question number one. Have you ever thought about me naked?" *Going straight for the kill it seems.*

"I... have not," I respond.

She releases a soft laugh. "Wow, this is easier than I

thought it would be." Her fingers find the hem of her shirt. "Your answer has been deemed a lie." She tugs the tank top off and tosses it to the floor.

"Judge, jury, and executioner, I see," I say, fighting the urge to take in the sight of her breasts, which are supported by a pretty black lace bra. *Fuck, they look as good as they tasted.*

"Question number two," she says, ignoring me. "Are you hard right now?"

I clench my jaw together because given how tight my jeans have gotten, she and I both know the answer to that question. "Nope."

"Tsk-tsk," she replies, stepping closer. "Shall we test that?"

I swallow hard as she invades my space, her sweet smell surrounding me like a walking Yankee candle. She rests a hand against my chest, and I suck in a breath, trying to think of anything that could kill this boner before she finds it. *Stinky football locker room... football locker room... football...* Nope, no use—brain's fried at her soft touch. Andi grabs my chin, forcing my eyes to meet hers as she glides her fingers down my abs to the hem of my pants.

"Let's see how honest you are, Porter," she taunts, sliding her hand over the bulge in my pants and grinning victoriously. "Yep, just as I thought."

She squeezes, and I fight a groan as she quickly releases, stepping away. "Your answer has been deemed a lie." She brings her hands to her waist and unbuttons her shorts before dropping them to the ground and kicking them off.

Matching black satin panties. Of course.

"Next question," she says, smiling, and my eyes rake over her. "What are you thinking about?"

Either way this goes, I'm fucked. My hands itch to touch her body, and if she drops another piece of fabric, I won't be able to stop myself. All that smooth skin on display. Her confidence. The way she calls out my bullshit and isn't afraid to take a little risk if it results in something we clearly both want.

This damn woman.

"You really wanna know?" I ask, stepping forward and caging her against the countertop.

"Either way, I'll end up naked," she says confidently, and fuck if it isn't the truest thing she's said all day.

I bend slightly, hooking my arms under her long legs, and she yelps as I hoist her up, setting her ass on the edge of the countertop. Positioning myself between them, I slide my fingers into her hair, tugging her head backwards to open up the column of her throat.

Dropping my mouth to her ear, I rasp, "I'm thinking about how I'm gonna punish you for being such a cock tease this past week. And that *maybe*, if you're a good fucking girl, I'll let you come by sinking into you till you see heaven. Then we can finally get it out of our systems so I stop feeling like my balls are gonna explode every time you walk in the damn room."

Her lips part open, fingernails digging into my shoulders, and she whispers, "Thank you for your candor."

I chuckle, dragging my lips against her neck. My hands rest on her thighs, gripping tight, giving me the last little illusion of my control.

"I think it's my turn to ask a question," I say.

"The answer is yes," she replies breathlessly.

"To which part?"

"All of it," she pants. "Fucking all of it."

My eyes connect with hers, swimming with lust. So hungry. So ready for me. She's confident and strong, but I know she'll melt in my hands like our kiss at the diner. I'm so sick of resisting this. Of holding us back from what we both want.

"Oh, for fuck's sake, Porter," she says, tugging me to her, and our lips crash, hands roaming one another's body in a panic. Our tongues tangle, and she throws her legs around me, heels digging into my ass, pulling me closer. She kisses like she's underwater and I'm her only source of oxygen. Like she'll die if she doesn't get one more. Hell, I know the feeling. *She tastes so good.* I kiss her lips, the side of her mouth, cheek, down to the side of her neck, nibbling lightly, and a soft moan escapes her. *Those sounds will be the death of me.* My hand wanders up her leg, and I dip a finger under the soft satin, drawing circles on the smooth skin of her hip.

I kiss down the center of Andi's chest, between the valley of her breasts, and reach around to unhook her bra. She tosses it off, and perfect pointed nipples stare at me. Taunting me. Begging for a taste. I slide my hand up her bare back and grip her hair. She moans when I suck a tit in my mouth, circling it with my tongue.

"I knew these would be as perfect as I imagined," I rasp against her skin.

"And I knew you'd look so fucking beautiful when you finally lost control," Andi coos.

"Don't be a brat." I bring my face to hers, lips drawing

closer with every breath. "We'll see who's begging for it soon."

"Don't come in your pants, Porter."

I pause and look up at her amused face. "Punishing you is gonna be so much fun." Sliding a hand between her legs, I cup her warm pussy. "And you'll be the one coming through your panties if I have anything to say about it."

16

ANDI

Porter presses against me, and I throb. He's not wrong. There's a high possibility he could make me come with my panties *on*. And some people can't even find your G-spot when spread eagle, buck naked, with a blinking arrow pointing to it.

"That's a lot of talk," I say. "You gonna back it up with an *actual* orgasm for proof of concept? Wanna set up a camera so I can give you pointers later? I know how much you coaches love watching your game tape."

"Don't tempt me," he growls against my breast. "I can assure you, we wouldn't be watching for review. It'd just be background noise for a repeat performance."

"Stop playing with your food," I taunt. "Go in for the kill."

He cocks a brow and takes a step back, eyes raking slowly over my body from head to toe like he's Nicolas Cage and I'm the mother fucking Declaration of Independence.

"You look so perfect. Spread your legs for me," he

instructs, taking another step back and leaning against the opposite counter with his arms folded across his chest.

"Excuse me?" I scoff, squeezing my thighs together to help ease the ache between them.

"Spread. Your. Legs," he repeats, and you know what? I'll happily play along so long as it ends with me sore and satisfied.

I slowly split them apart while placing my hands behind me to allow him an unobstructed view.

"Touch yourself," he instructs.

Nibbling on my lower lip, I contemplate him. If this man wants a show, he's gonna fucking get one. I dip a hand below the band of my panties and find my clit, rubbing over the sensitive spot.

"What now, Coach?" I ask breathlessly as I make an exaggerated effort to show him how good I feel.

A slow smile spreads across his face. "What would you do if you were alone right now?"

I shimmy my thong off and drop it to the ground, then spread my legs wide again. "You really wanna know?"

"The best way to pleasure a woman is to learn how she pleasures herself," he responds.

"Seems like good advice."

"So show me how you pleasure yourself, and I'll show you how I do it better."

I swipe between my legs and—dripping wet, just as I expected. My eyes meet Porter's, and I bring my fingers to my mouth, sucking off the juices. I brush down the center of my chest back to my pussy and circle my clit.

"To be honest," I say, "I'm never really alone. My best friends are always with me."

"Stella?" he asks, brows shooting to his hairline.

"No, my toys."

Porter smirks. "And what kind of toys would those be?"

"Something thick and long I can ride till I can't see straight."

Porter's jaw ticks, and I sink my fingers into my opening, letting out a deep moan. His hand grips my wrist, darkened eyes holding mine as he tugs them out and sucks them clean. He drops to his knees in front of me, grasps my thighs, and tugs me closer to bury his face between my legs. *Looks like my little strip tease was worth it.*

"Fuck," I say as he devours me, and when he dips two fingers inside, I scream out in pleasure.

Porter stands, hands flying to his waistband, and drops both layers to the floor. *Damn, I knew he'd have a pretty dick.* "Turn over, baby. Let me see your pretty ass in the air." I spin over, knees digging into the countertop, and he grips a cheek in each palm. "So perfect," he groans, swiping a finger between me. "So wet for me." I lay my body flat against the cold marble, widening my thighs to give him better access.

He holds my hips, tugging me closer to the edge, and wastes no time before nudging his hardened cock against me.

"Think you can handle it, Cupcake?" he taunts, and I glare at him over my shoulder.

"Think you can go more than ten seconds without *blowing* it?"

He grips my hip tightly. "I already told you, if I blow it, it'll be on purpose."

"That so?" I grin. "First one to come loses."

"Feels like a win to me."

MERRY MISCHIEF LIST

"Oh yeah? Well, the actual winner gets to pick the next list item. And the loser can't drag them off."

"What makes you assume I'll be the loser?"

"I feel you throbbing. You're begging for a release." I lean back, sinking onto him. "And I'm happy to give it to you."

"You're such a fucking brat," he groans, one hand gripping my ass, the other on my hip while he thrusts. "I told you I'd punish you." A slap lands on my ass cheek, ricocheting throughout the room, and I jump.

"Aww." I jut out my lower lip in a pout. "Sorry, but I've been a very *naughty* girl this year." He slides out of me, and I whimper at the loss.

"Turn over."

I flip to face him, and he bends down before tossing me over his shoulder, giving me the perfect view of his naked round ass as he walks towards the stairs.

"What are you doing?" I ask with a laugh and spank him.

"Winner gets to choose your next list item?"

"Yep."

"First one to come loses?"

"Yes."

"Great. I'm just making sure I win." His assuredness makes me uneasy in the most exciting way. A yelp escapes me as I fly through the air and land on his bed. When I glance up, Porter's staring at me, eyes appreciatively roaming over my body. He disappears into the closet and comes out a minute later with a small box.

"Are you about to murder me?" I ask.

He lets out a low laugh, then opens the box, pulling out a

121

satin blindfold. "You said you like to use toys?" A pair of handcuffs comes out next.

"Yeah, like a dildo or butt plug. Are you about to go full BDSM on me?"

"Am I freaking you out?" His tone is soft, slightly concerned, but the lust in his eyes is obvious.

Let me think... This delicious-looking hunk of a man wants to tie me up and make it his sole mission to give me an orgasm?

"God, no." I throw my head against the pillow. "Although I do feel like this is cheating."

He takes my hands, cuffing them above my head to the metal bed frame. I wiggle slightly to check how stuck I am, and it only increases my excitement when I realize I can't move. He takes the blindfold and places it securely on my head, shielding my view.

"They say when your sight is blocked, all the other senses are heightened," Porter whispers as his hot breath hits against my ear.

"Is that so?"

He trails his fingertips up my side, leaving goosebumps in their wake. "Mm-hmm. Now you're gonna eat my cock like a good girl."

"God, you're bossy," I tease as he crawls up my body and rubs his thick dick against my lips. I jut my tongue out slightly, moaning when a drip of pre-cum hits it.

"Now suck." He slides inside, and I obey like my damn life depends on it. This is the only chance I'll have to make him come first, and I'm gonna make it count. My eyes water as he hits the back of my throat, and I relax, allowing him to sink deeper.

"I knew that smartass mouth was good for something," Porter rasps.

He fucks my face, and I thrive on the moans dropping from his lips.

"Shit," he says, pulling out abruptly.

"What's wrong, *baby*?" I taunt. "Weren't you having a good time?"

"Yeah, you little vixen. I was one more deep throat away from forgetting this is a competition."

A soft laugh escapes me. "Never underestimate your opponent."

The familiar rip of a foil packet has my lips quirking upwards.

"Ready to lose?" he asks.

My aching pussy is screaming *yes*, but my competitive side craves the win.

Porter swipes between my legs, pressing against my entrance. "You're so pretty spread open and tied up," he says, low and gravelly. I drop my legs open wider, inviting him in, and he wastes no time before plunging deep inside me. I release a loud moan, and he drops down, sucking a nipple into his mouth. He swirls his tongue around the peak before pulling it between his teeth, proving he can be both nice and naughty.

"You seem like one of those girls who likes her pleasure mixed with a little pain." His hand creeps up my neck, trailing the column of my throat. "Are you?"

"If you're asking if you can give me a hand necklace, you have my blessing."

He presses a hand down on my windpipe, pounding into me, and my lips curve upward. Maybe I'm a masochist.

Maybe I'm actually insane, but Porter's right. I really do love it. Neck play. Ass play. Nipple play.

All of it.

He pulls my nipple into his mouth again, sucking harder. "Fuck," I moan.

The release is building, and every touch is bringing me closer to the edge. His kisses trail upward, lips landing on my collarbone, and he makes his mark on me. Thank god school's out because there's no way I can hide this. I find his shoulder with my lips, and he hisses when I bite down on it. *Why should he be the only one who gets to leave a mark?*

"Come on," I taunt, throwing my head back against the pillow. "At this rate, you'll come before me."

A guttural laugh escapes him. "Trust me, I'm perfectly capable of maintaining my composure."

He presses his lips to mine, tongue slipping into my mouth. The pressure of his hand on my neck, his dick deep inside of me, the taste of him—it's all too much.

Like a lit firecracker, every signal shoots off at once, and I moan loudly in pleasure. Porter continues as I ride out the wave of the orgasm until I'm nothing but a puddle beneath him. "You all done, Cupcake?"

I pant hard as he slows his thrusts. "Fuck you."

He laughs and increases his pace again. "Gladly."

Shortly after, his cock jerks against my inner walls, and he stills above me.

He pushes the blindfold off my eyes and stares down at me. "Looks like I'm the winner."

"Don't get used to it."

17

PORTER

"My grandma always said the key to good gingerbread dough is preparing it the day before," Andi tells me, kneading the mixture on the flour-covered kitchen counter.

"Sounds like a smart woman," I reply, using my thumbs to massage her pretty bruised-up neck. *I may have gotten a bit carried away with the hickies.*

"She is," Andi agrees, plopping the finished dough in a bowl and covering it with plastic wrap. "Usually I would've made it this morning, but *somebody* was distracting me all day."

"Since when are orgasms a distraction?" I spin her to face me and slide a hand into her hair, angling her mouth toward mine, relieved I can do it freely now that we've finally given into our attraction. I was wondering how Andi would feel this morning, but given she was the one who woke *me* up with a sunrise blowjob, it seems we're on the same page as of now. And we've been "getting it out of our systems" all day.

In the shower.

On the couch.

On the kitchen counter.

And now I'm scanning the room for another area we can christen.

"Since you used it as a method to delay me from completing important tasks," she says, interrupting my plotting. "Like the Christmas Eve tradition of preparing gingerbread dough." I scoop her up, placing her on the counter, and she bats at me with flour-covered hands. "Porter! You're making a mess."

"If you'd stop swatting, my kitchen wouldn't look like a broken snow globe," I point out.

"Oh, really?" She reaches behind her, then taps a flour-covered hand against my face, a small white puff surrounding us.

"You looking for punishment, little miss mischief?"

Andi bats her long dark lashes at me. "Whatever do you mean?" She slides a hand over my hard dick and gives it a soft squeeze. "Looks like *little* Coach is in the mood for some trouble."

"Little?" I scoff, cocking a brow. "You really wanna—" The doorbell rings, and I groan. "For fuck's sake."

"Want me to get it so you can"—Andi's eyes drop to my very obvious hard-on—"readjust yourself?"

"Considering I don't know who it is and you're not even supposed to be here? Hard no."

I walk to the front door, brushing the flour off my crotch on the way, fully prepared to tell some Christmas carolers to fuck off. I swing the door open, and a laugh rips out of me instead.

"Ho ho ho," Knox bellows, dressed head to toe in a Santa

outfit, sans beard, with a red velvet sack swung over his shoulder.

"What the hell are you wearing?" I ask, eyeing him with amusement.

He walks in, bells on his belt jingling with each step. "What the hell am *I* wearing?" He laughs, eyeing me suspiciously. "Why does it look like you just got a blowjob from the Pillsbury dough boy?"

I follow his gaze down to my pants still covered in flour. "I've been busy."

"Clearly," he snorts as I shut the door. "You banged the cheerleader."

"Hey, I never said that," I say as we walk towards the kitchen.

Turning the corner, I see Andi cleaning the marble counter, flour stuck in her hair. On her tits. Ass. Long legs. That neck.

"Really?" Knox asks with a deep chuckle, glancing back at me. "You can't tell me this hard ten is powdered up in your kitchen, and you haven't even considered showing her a good time?"

"Well, hello Santa baby," Andi says, eyeing Knox, as her warm laugh floods the room. "Since I know he tells you everything anyway, I'm happy to report good times have already been had."

"Attaboy," Knox says, tossing his red sack on the counter.

"In fact…" Andi's amused eyes find mine. "Did you set this up?"

"What?" I ask, furrowing my brows at her.

"Santa suit," she says, eyes appraising Knox hungrily

before flicking back to mine. "Gotta say, I'm surprised this is the list item you chose, especially after the elf incident."

"What I—" And then it clicks. *Blow Santa.* "I did *not* set this up."

"Set what up?" Knox asks, eyes bouncing between us.

"Well, I lost a bet last night," Andi supplies. "Which means Porter gets to choose the next item on the list."

"Oh," Knox says, obviously intrigued. "And the item you chose was?"

"Nothing yet," I say, waving him off. "She's just poking the bear."

Andi winks at me then asks, "So what's in the sack?"

"Special delivery," he announces, dumping out the contents, and a hundred tiny alcohol bottles bounce across the marble.

"Damn," Andi says, hopping up on the counter. "Trying to get your elves fucked up?"

"Very funny," he says, shooting a wink at her. "But no."

"It's my annual refill," I say, smiling from ear to ear.

"Ooh, the plot thickens," Andi says, eyes bouncing between us. "How'd this little tradition start?"

"When Porter and I started playing together," Knox says, "we weren't used to having money. We'd stay in these fancy ass hotels, and after a game, we'd come back hoping to take the edge off."

"But the hotel minibar prices were criminal," I chime in. "And Knox and I were done paying twelve bucks for an ounce of cheap bourbon."

"Yeah, if you're gonna splurge, it better be the good stuff," Knox says. "So after a Christmas Eve game in Chicago, we hit up the corner liquor store and bought a fuck ton of mini bottles. Went back to Porter's room and got absolutely smashed. And thus…" He waves his arm at the countertop. "The tradition was born."

"Stick it to the minibar," Andi says. "I love it."

I pick up a small bottle of Baileys and hand it to her. Knox and I each grab a little Jack Daniel's.

"Wait, why do you guys get the fun stuff?" Andi asks.

"My apologies," I say, plucking the bottle from her fingers and replacing it with a bottle of Jack. She gives me a smile of approval, and we twist off the tops.

"To new traditions," I say, tipping the bottle towards them.

"To new traditions," they repeat, and we all down the liquor.

"Alright, now go get changed into something jolly," Knox instructs. "We're going to Ploutos."

"Come on," I groan. "I thought you'd skip this year."

"And stay in to drink cheap liquor and watch sappy Hallmark movies? No," Knox says firmly.

"You're the one who brought the cheap liquor," I point out.

"It's *tradition*," he says, throwing a hand over his chest, feigning offense.

"And it's perfectly acceptable for a lazy Christmas Eve night in," I counter. *Not that I actually intend to be lazy. I have other very active plans.*

"Stop being so bah humbug," Knox groans, then narrows his eyes on Andi. "How have you domesticated him so fast?"

"Don't look at me," Andi says, throwing up her hands. "I'm always up for a night out."

"See?" Knox says, throwing his arm around her. "Even

Pop Tart's down. You and I both know you have the perfect outfit, so stop being such a buzzkill."

Andi snorts a laugh, and I glare at her. "What was that about?" I ask her, eyebrows raised.

"Seems the CBU boys aren't the only ones who've deemed you Coach Buzzkill," she says, fully amused.

"Oh, shut it," I say, narrowing my eyes on her.

"Now go clean up. Party starts in an hour," Knox instructs, nudging me and Andi towards the stairs.

"You still got your elf costume?" I ask her.

"Never leave the house without it," she teases, and I throw my arm around her shoulders.

"We may need a few minutes," I tell Knox as Andi smirks up at me. "Gotta shower and clean up this beautiful mess before we can get ready."

"If you take too long, you'll need to make room for a third," Knox calls after us.

"Don't make promises you won't keep," Andi teases.

Knox lets out a warm laugh. "Trust me, Pop Tart. I don't."

18

ANDI

"Damn," Knox says with a whistle as I come down the stairs. "If Santa's elves looked like you, I don't think Christmas could ever get done on time."

"Don't worry," I tease. "I have effective methods of ensuring Santa's productivity."

He lets out a low chuckle. "That so?"

"Yep," I reply, grabbing a bottle of water from the fridge. *I'm gonna need to hydrate if I wanna keep up with these guys tonight.*

"The princess not ready yet?" Knox asks.

"He'll be down in a few," I reply with a laugh. "So you and Porter met playing for Tampa?"

"Nope, freshman year of college."

"My mom always told me you make lifelong friends in college," I say. "I wasn't sure if it was really true once you move and move on."

"Honestly, Porter is one of the few I actually stayed in

touch with. We played four years at CBU and then both got drafted to Tampa. Now we're just kinda stuck together."

"That's sweet. It must have been hard for you after he got hurt."

"Yeah." Knox leans against the counter. "We still see each other a lot, but it isn't the same. Not many people have the opportunity to travel and play pro ball with their best friend."

"Aww, don't worry," Porter says, walking down the stairs. "Once you outlive your use at Tampa, I'll hire you as a defensive coach, and we can travel again like old times."

"How considerate of you," Knox says with a teasing glare.

My mouth is dry taking in Porter, who's wearing a two-piece suit splattered with a pattern of Rudolph, sans shirt, showing off his rippled stomach.

"Damn, Coach," I blurt.

Porter grins, straightening his shoulders. "Will it do?"

I open and close my mouth, struggling to find the right words. *I wish he could dress like this on game day. It would definitely increase ticket sales.*

"Who knew you bought impractical clothes too?" I finally say.

"I would say a festive holiday suit is entirely practical," Porter replies, brushing the shoulder of his jacket. "Always gotta be prepared for the inevitable costume party."

Knox scoffs. "What he's failing to mention is the awesome person who *bought* him the suit in the first place."

"Only because you wanted to match at the Barracudas holiday party last year," Porter points out.

"How would people have known you were my date if we didn't match?" Knox argues.

"I was *not* your date," Porter clarifies.

"*I* invited you. We went *together.* We matched suits—"

"Because you made us," Porter interrupts Knox, and I fight a smile as my eyes bounce between them.

"Aww, is he the Daddy Dom in your relationship?" I ask Porter.

He slides his hand around my neck, tugging my head back, and leans down, lips inches from mine. Heat pools between my thighs as I struggle for air. "Maybe if you're a good girl, you'll get to find out for yourself." He releases his hold on me. "Let's go, Cupcake."

Thirty minutes later, we're making our way through the crowded club. Looks like everyone got the costume memo because there are Santas, snowmen, and gingerbread people galore in here. We fit right in.

We arrive at what I assume is the VIP section given there's a bouncer with a clipboard posted out front. He looks like the type of guy who gets a hard-on saying no to people. His entire demeanor changes when he sees us, and I think, in fact, what he truly gets a hard-on from is seeing Knox because he practically drops the velvet rope as we arrive.

"Mr. Knox," the bouncer says, gesturing us inside.

"Thanks," Knox says, leading us to a small, cozy-looking couch toward the back of the room.

Porter and Knox sit on opposite ends, and there's just enough room for me to slide my body between them. The lights are dim, and even in the crowded space we have plenty of privacy. *Wouldn't mind taking advantage of it.*

A server arrives with a round of tequila shots. We knock them back, and it goes down smoother than a penguin on ice.

"Damn, that's good stuff," I say, setting my glass on the low table before us.

"One of my favorites," Knox says, leaning forward and brushing my bare leg as he sets his shot glass next to mine. He leans back, spreading his arm over the back of the couch, and I struggle to think straight as his red velvet jacket slides open, giving the perfect view of his exposed muscular stomach. *Do these men not own shirts?*

"It's a far cry from mini bottles of bottom shelf liquor," I say.

"Well, like I said earlier," Knox replies, "I don't mind paying for things *worth* the money. I just hate getting ripped off overpaying for cheap crap."

"Don't let him fool you. He's totally high maintenance," Porter teases, fingers brushing lazily along my thigh as a server replaces his shot glass with his standard glass of bourbon. They must come here often considering the servers bring their favorites without even being asked.

"It's not high maintenance to enjoy the finer things in life," Knox argues.

"I suppose that's true," Porter concedes, eyes sliding to mine before dropping to my lips. I cross my legs, squeezing them together to relieve a bit of pressure from the overwhelming testosterone surrounding me. "You okay there, Cupcake?"

"Peachy," I choke out. Glancing around, I wonder how many people in this place know the two men I'm with. "Are you not worried about us being seen together here?"

"Anyone who would recognize the both of us would definitely not be here tonight. And this place is phone free." Porter gestures to a sign on the wall. "It's a lot of celebrities and politicians coming here for a good time. Not to be recorded. They're pretty serious about it."

"Well, good thing you told me before I took a picture and got tackled by the bouncer," I sass.

"Aww, don't worry, Pop Tart," Knox says. "I would've intercepted him."

"How lucky am I?" I say, fluttering my eyelashes, and placing a palm over my heart.

"Considering you're spending Christmas Eve with the two of us?" he says, grinning at Porter. "I'd say you've been a pretty good girl this year."

"Is that so?" I ask, eyeing Knox's costume.

"Sure is. Come tell Santa what to bring you," he says, patting his thigh and gesturing for me to sit.

"The only thing you're capable of bringing is the twelve STDs of Christmas," Porter says, laughing deeply.

"Oh, fuck off, you know I'm Mr. Clean," Knox retorts, but his tone is lighthearted.

I lean back, bringing my mouth to Porter's ear. "Aww, didn't you ever learn to share?"

A warm laugh escapes him. "I can share. When I want to."

"Oh, really?" I ask, with a cocked brow. "So it wouldn't bother you if I slid onto his lap?"

Porter waves his hand, paired with an expression that says *be my guest.*

I turn back to Knox, snaking my arm around his neck, and he pulls me onto him, resting a warm hand on my thigh. "Don't worry, Porter," I say, rubbing my heeled feet against his leg, "you can have my feet. I know they're your favorite part anyway."

"Oh," Knox says, dragging a hand through my hair. "You've discovered his weakness then?"

"Hah! I knew it," I say, sliding my foot slowly up Porter's leg, and he grabs it, pausing my exploration.

"Brat," Porter says, his hand gliding up my ankle and calf, gaze heating me from the inside out as he smirks at Knox over my shoulder.

Knox shifts below me, and I don't know if it's just me, but it has gotten h-o-t in here. He brushes my hair to the side with his fingertips, then says, "So what do you want for Christmas, Pop Tart?"

19
PORTER

Andi's eyes find mine, a challenge behind them as she trails her hand up and down Knox's bare torso. I wait for the jealousy to come, but all that happens is I get fucking hard.

If it were any other guy, this is definitely the part where I'd tell them to back off. But things have never been that way between me and Knox. We've shared girls in the past, and I can't help but be curious how I'd feel about us sharing *her*. *Considering we're just getting this out of our systems.*

"Ask me again later," Andi says, arms hooked around his neck.

"Why?" Knox asks. "Afraid you'll change your mind?"

"*Ho ho ho,*" a voice says over the loudspeaker, grabbing our attention.

"What's going on?" Andi asks, and I point to my ear, gesturing for her to listen.

"'Twas the last twerk before Christmas, when all through Ploutos, the drinks were free flowing: shots, champagne, and cosmos. Everyone waited round the dance floor and stared, in hopes elves would soon shake their asses off there. One lucky winner will soon be snug in their bed, with five grand in cash tucked under their head. Come down to the dance floor so we can begin the search for the Last Twerk Before Christmas Champion!"

"Five grand?" Andi gawks, jumping off Knox's lap. "For a twerk contest? Sign me the fuck up."

"Why do you think it's so packed here tonight?" Knox says as we stand to join her. "There's nothing rich people love more than getting richer."

"Well, you know who loves winning money more than rich people?" Andi asks rhetorically. "Broke people. Looks like this elf's twerking for cash tonight." Knox and I share a look, and Andi's expression drops. "Are you guys gonna tell me not to do this? Because there's nothing wrong with—"

"That's not what we were gonna say," I assure her, placing my hand on her lower back. "You go twerk to your heart's content."

"Aren't you gonna join me?" She pouts, looking between us.

"Knox enters every year," I say. "But I'm a better coach than a player at these things, I promise."

"Okay, fine," she says, looking between me and the dance floor. "Think you could grab us another round of drinks? I'm gonna need a little jingle juice before getting low."

"You got it," I say. "One round of jingle juice coming up."

After a very tough twerk out, Knox and Andi were, unsurprisingly, invited on stage to take part in a lap dance contest between the last six remaining contestants.

We have Knox dressed as gigolo Santa, Andi the sexy elf,

a scandalous Ms. Claus, twins dressed as chestnuts, and a guy with Christmas ornaments and bells hanging off him. *A creative take on jingle balls.*

The Christmas version of "Pony" by Ginuwine is playing through the speakers as Knox performs his lap dance on all the contestants. When he gets to Andi, he holds himself in a handstand and slowly grinds down against her. Andi's laughing hysterically, the crowd's going wild, and it's clear he came to win. Even I've gotta admit he'll be a tough act to follow.

After his song ends, he and Andi switch places, and she starts with his lap first to the tune of "Christmas Lap Dance" by R-DOT. The DJ should get a raise because these back tracks are hilariously perfect. Andi's body sways in perfect rhythm to the music as she glides her tight ass against Knox's front. His eyes connect with mine, and the look on his face tells me he'd much rather be getting this show in private. *That makes two of us.*

After a heated battle, a redhead dressed as Ms. Claus ends up beating them both with a very sexual rendition of "Santa Baby" that practically puts half of Ploutos in a blue-ball-induced coma.

Knox and Andi walk off the stage with glowing smiles and heads held high.

"Sorry you didn't win," I tell Andi, tucking her under my arm.

"That's alright," she says, beaming up at me. "It was a blast."

"I'm pretty sure Knox almost lost the deposit on his Santa suit for how good your performance was," I tell her, cocking a brow at him.

"Oh, please," he says with a laugh. "No need to worry about my deposit. I bought this suit."

"Of course you did," I say.

"I still can't believe my Magic Santa routine didn't win first place." He shakes his head.

"Aww, don't worry," Andi says, patting his chest. "Channing Tatum would've been proud."

"There's always next year, buddy," I tease, and he flips me off.

"Yeah, and if the football thing doesn't work out, I think you'd make a killing at Chippendales," Andi supplies.

"It *is* always good to have a back-up plan," Knox agrees just as the redhead who won the contest walks up to us.

"Hey, y'all," she says with a sweet smile.

"Congrats, Felicity!" Andi says, pulling her into a hug.

"Thanks," Felicity says. "I think you were robbed though."

"Girl, shut up. You slayed," Andi replies genuinely. "A Nonsense Christmas" by Sabrina Carpenter comes over the loudspeaker, and Felicity's face lights up.

"Oh, I love this song!" she says, bouncing energetically and grabbing Andi's hands. "Please dance with me? I'm so wound up from the contest."

"Later, boys," Andi says, shooting me a wink before being dragged onto the dance floor.

I struggle to pull my eyes away as Andi sways her hips to the beat. Knox throws his arm around my shoulder, drawing my attention to him.

"You look like a perv in a closet at a girls' slumber party, bro. Let's go get a drink," he says, and I glare at him.

"You're such a dick sometimes."

He chuckles, dragging me away. "Come on."

We settle at the bar, fresh drinks in hand.

"So it seems you and Andi are getting along pretty well," he says.

"We're just blowing off steam," I say, trying to convince the both of us.

"Yeah, sure." Knox takes a swig of his drink. "Seems you've got an awful lot of steam to blow."

"What can I say?" I grin. "The girl's got a lot of energy." Andi's like the fucking energizer bunny. Her rebound time to handle another orgasm is impressive. *And I'm enjoying testing those limits very much.*

"She's amazing, man," Knox says, leveling me. "Just admit you like her."

"You seemed to enjoy her company just as much," I point out.

"Like I said, she's awesome." He tips his drink towards me. "And ridiculously hot."

I clink my glass against his. "You're not wrong."

"Hey," Andi says, popping between us and throwing her arms over our shoulders. "Felicity's buying me a drink," she tells me, waggling her eyebrows. "We might have a shot for the triple gumdrop tonight!" She smacks a kiss on my cheek before slipping away again, and I can't wipe the stupid smile off my face.

Does the idea of her and a sexy southern redhead in my bed turn me on? Sure. But watching Andi enjoying herself, being confident in her own skin and sexuality, that's attractive as hell.

"You seem awfully happy at the mention of a holiday candy," Knox says with a cocked brow.

I take a swig of my drink. "It's a very delicious candy."

"The kind that gets you laid?" he presses.

"Indeed." I smirk, filling him in on the dirtier details of Andi's list while keeping track of her in my peripheral.

A tall, muscular guy with tattooed arms the size of my head walks up to them. He's not in costume and looks like he should be bouncing for a biker bar instead of hanging out in this place. He leans down to Felicity, and she plants a big kiss right on his lips. *Interesting turn of events.*

"Dude," Knox says, snapping in front of my face. "Are you even listening to me?"

"Hold on," I wave him off, trying to gauge what's going down at the end of the bar. The guy gives Andi an appreciative once-over, his arm slung loosely over Felicity. I can only see the back of Andi's head, but I can tell by the way her shoulders shake she's laughing.

"Ohhh, I see," Knox says, following my line of sight. "You're worried she's gonna complete the triple gumdrop without you."

"What?" I scoff. "She wouldn't."

"Why not?" Knox presses. "It's not like you're exclusive."

"I know, but we're…" *Hooking up? Fucking?* "Getting it out of our systems."

"Famous last words," Knox says, patting my back with a laugh.

I roll my eyes, attention turning back to Andi, but she's gone. As are the gigantic bouncer and Felicity. *Shit.*

"Well, maybe they took her up on that offer," Knox says like the asshole he is.

"Over my dead body," I say, pushing away from the bar

and starting towards the place I last saw them. I'm halfway to the spot when a hand grips my elbow, stopping me in place.

"Whatcha doing, Coach?" Andi asks, staring up at me expectantly.

"Me? What are *you* doing?"

"Looking for you?" she says with a puzzled look on her face.

"Here I am," I say, blood lowering back to a simmer.

"Are you okay?" she asks, taking both my hands and pulling me towards the dance floor. She places them on her waist and hooks her arms around my neck. "You look tense."

"What happened to your new friends?"

She cracks a knowing smile. "Well, Felicity was a hundred percent on board with the triple gumdrop."

"And?" I press.

"And so was her husband."

I nod my head. "So are you asking for permission or…?"

"I wasn't aware I needed it," she says with raised brows.

"You don't."

"Well, for the record, I'm not interested in having a threesome you're not involved in."

"Oh, really?" I ask in surprise.

"At least not tonight," she clarifies. "I know we're not, like, exclusive or dating or whatever, but we still have two more days before practice starts back up, and I'd much rather you be the one coming down my chimney."

"Wow," I say, dropping my forehead to hers. "So romantic."

"What can I say?" she says, nuzzling my nose. "I'm a bit of a wordsmith."

A deep laugh escapes me. "You should make Hallmark cards."

"Merry Christmas; let's fuck until we can't walk."

"I'd buy that one for sure," I say, trying to ignore how turned on I am right now. "Wanna get out of here?"

"I thought you'd never ask."

Mariah Carey plays through the speakers, and Andi sings along, dancing around the living room with a big smile on her face. She changed into my old Tampa Barracudas jersey, and every time she throws her hands up, the hem rises a few inches, giving the perfect view of her long legs. *She's exquisite.* My gaze turns to Knox, who's sitting in his Santa pants with suspenders, sans jacket. I smile to myself as he enjoys Andi's playfulness as much as I do.

"You guys really gonna make me dance alone?" Andi asks, facing us with a teasing grin.

Knox's eyes connect with mine, and I tilt my head, gesturing for him to join her. He gets off the couch, and Andi winks at me. Knox grabs her hands and spins her around before pulling her closer to him. He leans down, whispering something in her ear, and she laughs. *Fuck, that laugh is so pretty.*

Andi grinds her ass against him while smirking at me, the heat in her gaze drawing me in like a siren song. She feels in control, which is sexy as hell. But it's my turn to call the shots.

"Knox, I'm gonna need you to strip," I say.

"Oh, really?" Andi asks, eyes wide and full of amusement.

"At least buy me dinner first," Knox says, making a show of slowly sliding the suspenders off his shoulders.

"It's time to mark another item off your list," I tell Andi, standing up and unbuttoning my reindeer dress pants, dropping them to the floor.

"And what would that be?" Andi asks, eyes glued to my very visible hard-on.

"Isn't it obvious?" I say, gesturing to Knox's costume.

"You want me to blow Santa?" Andi asks, eyes swinging back to Knox as he kicks off the red velvet pants.

"Yep," I say, snatching them off the ground.

"Really, man?" Knox says, groaning in annoyance. "It's *my* costume."

"Don't worry." My eyes bounce between them before settling on Knox. "You can watch."

20

ANDI

"You're such a dick," Knox says with a laugh as Porter finishes putting on the Santa costume.

"Don't hate the player," Porter says, winking at him.

Knox takes Porter's place on the couch, wearing nothing but sexy Prada boxers.

"You guys are concerned about the cost of hotel minibars, but you wear designer boxers?" I ask Knox, eyes glued to the very well-endowed package hidden beneath them. *Now that's a present I'd be happy to unwrap.*

"It's the principle behind it," Knox says, bringing my focus back to his piercing eyes. *Damn, is he pretty.* My attention slides to Porter looking like a holiday stripper I'd drop a grand on to give me a lap dance. *Fuck, he's pretty.*

"So you never told us," Porter says as my eyes slide between the finest pieces of ass I've ever seen. "What do you want for Christmas?"

Dear Santa, all I want for Christmas is to get absolutely railed by the two hot as hell, half-naked men before me.

"I think I'd rather you decide," I say, and Porter and Knox share a look.

I am in so much damn trouble.

"On your knees, Cupcake," Porter commands, and my knees hit the carpet. Because when a six-foot-three football coach looking like Santa's gift to women tells you to, you fucking listen.

"That's our good girl," Knox coos from the couch, and his approval increases my eagerness tenfold. Porter's always so wound up, like every move he makes is calculated. Maybe he was afraid I couldn't handle a man who knows what he wants. And knowing he likes to have an audience? Icing on the damn cupcake.

I hook my fingers onto the hem of the velvet pants and tug them, along with his boxers, down, dropping them to his ankles. *Looks like Santa's delivering cock after all.*

"You've been a naughty girl," Porter says, low and gravelly.

"Well, let me show you just how *nice* I can be," I say, taking his thick length in my hand. His fingers grip my hair, and I lick a bead of pre-cum off the tip, moaning from the sweet taste.

Porter thrusts his hips, cock sliding between my lips. He yanks my hair, forcing me to look up at him. A dazed, horny smile spreads across his face. "Look at you, pretty girl. Taking me so well."

My eyes well with tears as he hits the back of my throat, and I hum around him, knowing how insane it drove him last night. I glance to Knox, who's watching in admiration, tight boxers showing how *strong* his admiration is. Clenching my legs together, I try to suppress the throbbing between them.

But it's no use; the ache is insatiable. I need something. Anything.

I flick my tongue around Porter's shaft, moving my hand up the length I can't take in my mouth, and deep moans escape him. He tugs me upwards by my hair, and I release him with a pop to stand.

"Now you can mark 'Blow Santa' off your list," Porter says, stroking himself with a lazy smile. He stands behind me and turns to face Knox, who's still watching appreciatively from the couch. Porter slips his hands under the hem of his jersey I stole and pushes it up to my hips, revealing my soaked satin green panties. "Knox, we'll need your assistance for the next item. If you can handle it."

"Care to fill me in, Pop Tart?" Knox asks, eyes trailing me from head to toe. My skin is on fire from the undivided attention, and I'm struggling for air.

"Well," I say breathlessly, "I don't know if Porter told you about the triple gumdrop."

"He might have mentioned it," Knox replies, smirking at Porter over my shoulder as he slowly slides the jersey up my body, revealing more skin.

Porter drops his mouth to my ear. "Is it only for your list? Or have you actually fantasized about having us together?"

"Can't it be both?" I reply as his warm breath hits my neck, causing goosebumps to scatter across my body. He tugs the jersey off and tosses it to the ground, leaving me in nothing but my matching bra and panties.

"Come here," Knox says, crooking a finger in my direction, and I step forward, placing my palms on his firm shoulders. His warm hands grip my hips, guiding me onto him, and I straddle his lap. My aching pussy lands directly on his hard, throbbing cock, and I grind against it. "We're gonna make a mess of you tonight," he says, and I shiver at the promise.

Porter sits on the other end of the couch with the same hungry gaze he had during my lap dance performance. The appraisal brings out the cheerleader in me, and we love to put on a good performance.

I slide my hair to the side, exposing my neck, knowing it'll drive him nuts if Knox takes a taste. Sensing my offer, Knox pulls my body closer, pressing a kiss against my collarbone before venturing to my throat. He sucks hard, and I whimper, head falling back. His muscular arms hold my body firmly against him as I melt like butter under his touch. His kisses trail downward, and he wastes no time before leaving his own mark. He reaches a hand around and unclips my bra. I shimmy it off and chuck it behind me.

"How're you doing, Cupcake?" Porter asks. "We scare you off yet?"

"If you think I'm leaving before one of you has graced me with an orgasm," I say, eyes connecting with his as Knox devours my breast, "then you obviously don't know me very well."

Knox grips me by my ass and stands, turning to place me back on the couch. His knees hit the ground before me, and he places an ankle of mine on each of his muscular shoulders. He hooks a finger under my panties and begins slowly dragging them down.

"No," Porter says firmly. "Teeth."

Knox chuckles softly, then bends down, taking the fabric of my panties between his teeth. This clearly isn't the first time they've shared, and I've gotta admit, their ability to communicate with barely saying anything turns me the fuck on.

"You guys really know how to read each other, huh?" I pant out.

"That's what happens when you play on a team with someone for years," Porter says pointedly, rubbing a hand over his hardened cock.

"You learn highly effective threesome communication?" I ask.

"Among other things," he replies.

Knox's stubble scratches against my leg as he tugs my panties down and off, eyes glued to the place between my legs.

"What a pretty pussy," Knox purrs in approval.

"Taste," Porter instructs, watching smugly from the other side of the couch.

"Did you lose the ability to form sentences?" I tease, eyes locking with Porter's. He cocks a brow at me at the same moment Knox's tongue makes contact with my clit. "Oh…" I sigh, head falling back against the couch, and Knox grips my thighs. Fingers toy with my opening, and I glance down to see Porter's joined Knox on the floor. He's stretching me as Knox continues driving me insane with soft kisses.

Porter slides two fingers in, and I whimper. "Let's get you all nice and ready for us."

They continue their torment, and as I get close, which I'm sure is blatantly obvious by the sounds escaping my mouth, they both stop and stand abruptly.

"What?" I whine.

"I want you to come on my cock, Cupcake," Porter says.

"Then we can talk about continuing that *specific* form of pleasure. Now stand up."

My body is jello, but I find the strength to push myself off the couch. I slide between the two delicious and clearly very horny men, their hard dicks pressing against me from each side. Knox places his hands on my waist, turning me to face Porter. He grazes his teeth against my neck and bites down. I whimper, but the sound is swallowed by Porter's mouth on mine. He slides his tongue between my lips while his hands slide around, gripping my ass.

I'm so turned on I could come from the thought.

Knox snakes a hand around and rubs against my clit, causing my knees to buckle slightly. I hook my arms around Porter's neck and tug him closer, his hard cock pressing against Knox's hand for added friction.

I wonder if they're down for swordplay.

"Strip naked," I mumble into Porter's mouth. "Both of you."

They each release a single hand from me, and I swear I've never seen two men get butt ass naked so damn fast. I glance behind me, eyes connecting with Knox. "Sit," I tell him, gesturing towards the couch. He takes a seat, spreading his legs wide, and his dick is as glorious as I imagined.

"Who's the bossy one now?" Porter says with a chuckle.

"You gonna punish me for that?" I ask.

Before I can blink, he has me bent over, face pressed against the couch. I yelp as a stinging slap comes against my ass. He tugs me back up and drops his mouth to my ear. "It's not punishment if you enjoy it." I clench my thighs together. "Now get on all fours in front of Knox. I know you've been craving to taste him."

I do as I'm told, and Knox slides closer to the edge, giving me the perfect angle. Porter drops down behind me, and I tremble when he swipes his cock between my legs. I reach out, taking Knox's dick in my hand, stroking slowly. A bead of pre-cum sits on the tip, and I smirk, swiping my thumb over it. I angle towards Porter and hold my finger out for him.

"Suck," I command.

"I'm not sure when you got the impression you were in charge," Porter says, gripping my ass firmly.

"Did I stutter?" I ask, hovering my finger directly over his lips. His gaze flicks behind me with a cocked brow.

"You heard her," Knox says, rubbing a hand up my other arm lightly. "Do it."

The corner of Porter's lip twitches, eyes connecting with mine, and I suck in a breath as he takes my finger into his mouth.

"Such a good boy," I coo, and Porter's heated gaze sears into me. *I'm in so much trouble.*

"That's enough talking from you," Porter says, grabbing my hair and wrapping it around his hand. "Now it's your turn." He guides my mouth toward Knox, and I part my lips to finally taste him for myself.

These men and their delicious dicks.

I take Knox deeper, and a moan breaks free as Porter slides inside of me. His gentle thrusts allow the perfect rhythm for Knox to face fuck me.

Who the hell wants to be on the nice list if this is what being naughty gets you?

Porter hits that perfect place inside of me, and I grip

Knox's muscular thighs tightly, nails digging in as I give him the sloppiest blowjob known to mankind.

Giving head while your pussy gets obliterated is not a perfect art form. And I'll admit this is a first for me. Although hopefully not the last.

"Look at you taking us so well," Knox purrs, sliding his hands along my shoulders and down to cup my breasts. "Our perfect girl."

"So warm and tight," Porter groans. "I'm getting close."

"Wow," Knox taunts. "You're gonna finish before she's even come once? A bit selfish, don't you think?"

"Oh, she'll get the favor returned tonight between the two of us, don't *you* think?" Porter says, the promise causing a shiver of excitement through me.

A warm chuckle leaves Knox, and there's something so innately comfortable about how they talk to each other while inside me. It makes the whole thing indescribably more pleasurable. There's no awkwardness or jealousy, just three people enjoying each other.

Porter increases his pace, making it hard to maintain my mouth's position. Knox slides his fingers into my hair and tugs me up to his eye level, pulling my mouth to his, our tongues tangling. He kisses me breathless and slides a hand down, then rubs my clit while Porter grips my hips.

A loud moan escapes me, which Knox swallows as I come so hard my entire body trembles. Goosebumps trickle down my spine, and Porter twitches inside, coming shortly after me. I collapse against Knox, and he rubs his fingers lightly down my back as Porter pulls out of me.

"See, the score's one to one," Porter says triumphantly. "Your turn."

"I might…" I pant. "I might need just a… a minute."

Porter laughs, standing and holding the filled condom on his dick. "I'm gonna clean this up." His eyes hold mine. "Catch your breath, Cupcake. But we're not done with you yet."

I turn toward Knox, and the look of hunger on his face has me rallying faster than a tire change on an F1 race car. He holds my hips as I use all my remaining strength to straddle directly over him. Knox flinches as a condom hits him in the face.

"Don't forget, she's still mine," Porter says, tone firm. "If somebody's gonna come inside her, it's gonna be me first."

Porter leaves for the bathroom, and I laugh, grabbing the condom and rolling it onto Knox. A shudder escapes me as I lower myself onto him.

"You okay there, Pop Tart?" he asks.

"I think I can rally." I smirk.

"Attagirl." He presses his lips to mine, and I grip his shoulders, thrusting with vigor to chase another orgasm.

Porter reenters the room, grinning hungrily when he sees me. "I knew you could take it," he tells me, coming to stand behind the couch, placing his hands on Knox's shoulders. "You both look so good, fucking wild like this." He bends down to Knox's ear and whispers something, causing Knox to grip my waist tightly, fingernails digging in.

"Keeping secrets, you two?" I tease.

Porter's gaze locks with mine. "I told him if he doesn't make you come again, he'll be the next one punished."

He maintains eye contact while dropping his mouth to plant a kiss along the side of Knox's neck, and my eyes widen slightly in surprise, in arousal. Knox drops his head back against the couch, giving Porter better access. Porter slides his hands down Knox's chest, finding mine, and I lean forward, running my tongue up the opposite side of Knox's neck. A low groan escapes Knox as Porter and I make our mark on him while holding on to each other.

Knox wraps his arms around me and quickens his pace. The feeling of his cock inside me, Porter's touch, Knox's grip on my body, the taste of Knox's skin against my tongue—it's an out of body experience. I don't just come. I fucking erupt, every muscle in my body shaking, trembling as they make a volcano out of me.

Knox's low moans fill my ear, and we tumble together until I finally collapse against him. Porter rubs a hand over my hair, kissing me on top of the head. "I think I might be a fan of the triple gumdrop."

"Yeah?" I say breathlessly. "Me too."

"Me three," Knox agrees.

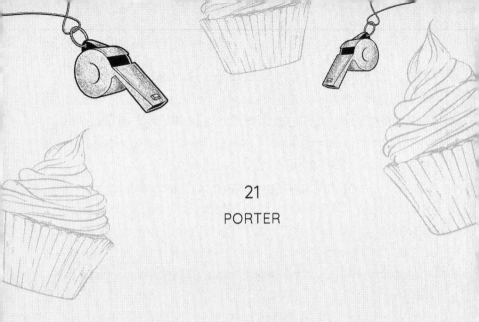

21

PORTER

"Good morning," I tell Andi, whose limbs are flung over me as we struggle to pull ourselves out of bed.

"Five more minutes," she groans, tugging closer to my naked body. Usually I'm a compulsive early morning riser, but judging by the light streaming through the blinds, it's at least nine.

"If you don't get up soon, I might have my breakfast in bed," I tease, dragging a hand up her thigh.

"I can't believe I'm saying this," Andi mumbles into my side. "But I don't know if I can handle another orgasm."

"Oh, come on, Pop Tart," Knox says, walking through my bedroom door, three mugs of coffee in hand. "Didn't you say, and I quote, 'I think I can rally'?"

"Yeah." Andi sits up and takes a mug. "About six orgasms ago."

"Seven if you count the double orgasm you had during the shower," I correct, pleased at how absolutely filthy our night went last night. I'm not sure where this goes from here, but in our little happy holiday bubble, I wouldn't be opposed to an annual triple gumdrop.

Knox resumes his place next to Andi, and we all settle in against the headboard.

"So, I thought I should warn you guys," Knox says, his tone hesitant.

"What's wrong?" I ask. *What the hell could he be so nervous to tell us?*

"Nothing's *wrong*, per se," Knox replies, pulling out his phone and handing it to me.

"What do you—" A picture of Knox with his arm around Andi as we left the club last night displays on the screen. I'm on the opposite side with my head turned so you can't tell it's me. There's another photo of Andi giving Knox a lap dance during the costume contest. The headline reads, *Knox'ing Boots for the Holidays? Kensington Knox and Mystery Girl Enjoying Christmas Eve at Ploutos Night Club.*

"How the hell do these photos even exist?" I ask, sitting up straight. *I knew better than to go in public with Andi.*

"If you were the paparazzi, where would you go for a hot story?" Knox says. *To the one place people would never expect.*

"Wait, so I did a holiday costume contest with you, and they just assume we banged?" Andi says.

"We *did* bang," Knox reminds her with a boop to the nose.

"Yeah, but they don't know that," she says.

"I know," Knox says, placing his hand on her thigh. "But that's what the paps do. They take one out of context picture and add some bullshit story for views."

I scroll through the article, scanning for any mention of

my name. It's one thing for Andi to be seen with Knox. They can brush it off as a good time, but if I'm connected to this…

"Don't worry, the article doesn't mention you," Knox says, reading my mind as always.

"Not at all?" I ask.

"Not a single time," he assures me, and I lean back against the headboard. "And Andi's name isn't mentioned. Only someone who recognizes her face could know it's her."

"Well, I guess that's good," Andi says, glancing at me.

"Yeah," I say, leaning back against the pillows. *But it could've been bad. Really bad.*

"It is good," Knox says. "And it'll blow over in a few days. If anyone asks, Andi and I met at Ploutos. We had a good time. There's nothing more to tell."

Andi rests a hand on my arm. "As long as we're all fine with that."

"Yeah, of course," I reply. "It's the best explanation for all of us."

"Agreed," Andi says. "Now that's settled, what's on the agenda for today?"

"Well, what's left on your little list, Ms. Mischief?" Knox asks. *Besides almost blowing up my life?* I force myself to shake off any remaining negative thoughts.

"Well, I never got to do the elf licking whipped cream off my tits thanks to this confusing, jealous asshole," Andi says, glaring at me, and I shut her up with a kiss. "So the last *possible* item is the gingerbread man cookies. Which is great because I definitely need the carbs. Wanna join?"

"As fun as that sounds," Knox says, "some of us actually have to visit family for Christmas."

"Booo," Andi grumbles.

"You guys are welcome to join. My parents always make plenty," Knox offers.

"I don't think I could be in the same room as your mother after what we did last night," Andi says. "Can you imagine? Oh, hey, Andi, how do you and Knox know each other?" she says, presumably impersonating Knox's mom. "Well, he face fucked me while his best friend railed me from behind."

"You know," Knox says, placing his hands on the bed and bending down to Andi's eye level. "I think that's more of a don't ask, don't tell type of situation." He kisses her, then walks towards the door.

"Merry Christmas!" Andi says. "And thanks for the orgasms."

"Same time next year?" Knox teases.

"Definitely," Andi and I chime in unison.

"Okay, this one's damn near perfect," Andi says, and I walk over to see her cookie craftsmanship.

A loud laugh escapes me as I stare down at a gingerbread man with a giant dick and balls. "What the hell is that?"

"It's a gingerbread man," she says casually.

"Okay, and what's between its legs?"

"Have you never seen a dick before? I would've thought you at least snuck a peek at Knox's last night."

"Okay, smartass," I say, spanking her, and she yelps. "But why does your cookie have one?"

"Didn't you read the list?" I stare at her in confusion, and she pulls it out.

Gingerbread man cookies. XLGD.

"I'm not computing."

"Gingerbread man cookies," she says like I'm stupid. "Extra. Large. Ginger. Dick."

"Wow, I really have no clue about the acronyms used these days. I don't know past LOL or LMAO."

"Learn something new every day, old man," she says, patting my chest and putting the cookies in the oven.

After we've eaten our weight in Dragon Wok and had gingerbread man cookies, *and their dicks*, for dessert, we settle into the couch and Andi forces me to watch *The Grinch*.

About a half hour in Who-ville, I reach next to the couch, grabbing the tiny bag I hid earlier. "I have something for you."

"Really?" She perks up, pausing the movie. "You didn't need to get me anything."

"I know," I say, handing it to her. "But I saw it at the mall, and it reminded me of you, so I wanted you to have it."

She pulls the tissue paper out and unwraps her gift. A small pink rocking horse ornament rests in her palm, and her sweet laugh fills the room. Her warm eyes find mine, and she shakes her head. "Thank you."

"It's nothing," I say, shifting in my seat.

"It's not a house key, Porter," Andi says, smiling softly. "But it's not nothing. *Thank you.*"

"You're welcome," I say, and she presses a warm kiss to my lips.

"I'll be right back," she tells me, and goes to the kitchen.

A few minutes later she returns, two glasses of red wine

in hand and a coy smile on her face. I stand and take a glass from her.

"I wanted to thank you for making sure my Christmas didn't suck," she says, tipping the glass towards me.

"I think the only one sucking this Christmas was *you*," I point out, and she rolls her eyes as we clink glasses.

"Technicalities," she teases, taking a sip and grabbing the remote to pull up YouTube on the smart TV. "I Saw Mommy Kissing Santa Claus" comes over the speaker.

"Care to dance?" she asks, and I pluck the wine from her hand, then set our glasses on the coffee table and tug her to the middle of the room. I take one hand in mine and settle the other on her waist while she rests her free hand on my shoulder.

I glance into her beautiful eyes, wondering how the hell I'll be able to forget the way she's looking at me right now.

"You're harder to get out of my system than I thought you'd be," I admit. *We're supposed to be blowing off steam, not catching feelings.*

"Back at ya, Coach," Andi says, resting her head on my chest. "So I guess tomorrow is our last day before we head back to reality and pretend this never happened?"

Because that's going to be so easy. "It's probably for the best."

"Yeah, I know."

"Especially after the article," I remind her. *That stupid damn article could've put me in deep shit.*

"I realize it probably would have been bad if you were recognized," Andi says.

"It definitely wouldn't have been ideal."

"Well, how about this: we spend the rest of our time

really, and I mean *really*, getting it out of our systems. And then at practice, you can go back to forgetting I exist and try not to think about what I taste like or the little sounds I make." She smiles playfully, and I tap my forehead to hers.

"You're not gonna make this easy, are you?" I ask, already picturing her naked and spread out for me.

"Maybe, maybe not." She shrugs.

"I'll manage, but do you think you'll be able to look at me across the field without remembering how my tongue made your legs shake?"

Her jaw tightens. "Looks like two can play at this game."

"I play to win, Cupcake."

"Then game on, Coach."

22
ANDI

The field is buzzing with energy as the Crystal Bay football players complete their warm-up. With the bowl game only a few days away, us cheerleaders will practice alongside them until we leave for Arizona. It feels good to be back, but I'd be lying to say I didn't wish I was still in a certain coach's bed.

I pull my arm across my body, trying to get loose, while my eyes drift to the sidelines where Porter stands, arms folded and a clipboard in his hand. *Why must he always look so damn sexy?* I curse myself for being weak as flashbacks of the last few days pound through my head. I taunted him about being unable to forget our attraction, but it's the first day back, and all I can think about are his hands on my waist, nails digging in as he—

"*Hellllloooo!*" Fingers snap in front of my face. "Earth to Andi!"

I shake my head to refocus on the present and see Stella's smiling face.

"Well, hey there, stranger," I say, pulling her in for a big hug. "I was wondering if you were gonna make it."

"Yeah, our flight got delayed, so we came straight from the airport," she says, looking toward the field. "I'm sure Theo's gonna get in some deep shit for that."

"Who knows," I say. "Maybe Coach will be a little lenient since it's the first day back."

"Unlikely," Stella says with a laugh, starting her warm-up stretch. "So are you gonna tell me about him?"

Was my staring too obvious?

"About who?" I ask casually.

"Are you kidding me?" Stella scoffs. "You're really gonna hold out on me?"

"Sorry, it's been a long week, you're gonna have to be more specific."

She lowers her voice to a whisper. "How about the fact you were *Knox'ing* boots with Kensington Knox!"

"That's hearsay." I smirk.

"Oh, come on." Stella rolls her eyes. "I saw the article. Please tell me he helped you mark off 'Blow Santa'?"

"I plead the fifth."

"Since when are you so stingy with the sexy details?" she whines.

"Fine," I concede, knowing Knox and Porter agreed to let it be the cover story. "Knox may have helped me complete an item or two off my list."

"Oh my god, I knew it!" she squeals. "How was he? Does he bang as good as he blocks?"

"Better," I tell her honestly, heat pooling between my thighs at the thought.

"You're so lucky." She sighs.

"So what about you? What was your final tally?"

"You first," she insists.

"I completed the entire Merry Mischief List except for one."

"Phew! Me too," she says with a laugh. "Let me guess, you couldn't block Olivia?"

"I *definitely* blocked her," I say pointedly. *I haven't thought about her in days.* "It was the elf licking whipped cream thing."

"What? That was easy! I did it on the first day."

I shrug. "Something got in the way. What didn't you complete?"

She twists her mouth. "Take a wild guess."

"Blow Santa?"

"Listen, if Kensington Knox had been before me in his Santa suit, I would've checked that item off too."

"Mm-hmm, excuses, excuses."

"So what does that mean for the Arizona streak?" Stella asks.

"Looks like we're both getting naked."

23
PORTER

Glendale, Arizona – New Year's

"I can assure you it won't happen again," I tell the front desk receptionist, blood reducing to a simmer. As if the day weren't stressful enough, a few of the guys thought it was a good idea to throw a party in their tiny hotel room and, of course, there were noise complaints. Luckily, I was able to talk the hotel out of calling the cops.

"Thank you, Mr. Porter," he replies.

"Please let me know if there're any further issues," I tell him. "I'll handle them directly."

"Yes, sir," he says. "And congratulations on winning the Desert Bowl."

"Thank you," I say and walk away towards the elevators, reflecting on the day. Winning was for damn sure a career highlight, but the aftermath definitely was not.

There's a buzz under my skin that has me feeling a little reckless tonight. As much as I've tried to convince myself

Andi and I can go back to being strangers, pretending we didn't spend last week making merry mischief, I think I've severely underestimated my willpower.

The past few days have been absolute torture. Every time her eyes landed on me, it was like I could feel her saying, *I know what you look like naked.* And then I'd picture her stripped bare and spread wide, ready for me.

I glance out the glass front doors and spot a CBU football hoodie. Blowing out a heavy breath, I make my way outside into the chilly Arizona night air.

Theo Schroeder stands on the edge of the parking lot, holding some type of towel in his hands. I clear my throat, and his head whips in my direction, eyes wide as saucers.

"Uh, hey, Coach," he sputters as I check my watch.

1:12 a.m.

"I know it's New Year's Eve, but may I remind you we're still on a school-affiliated trip, which means curfew was twelve minutes ago."

"I'm..." He darts his eyes toward the sidewalk. *Waiting on someone?* I want to ask but opt to keep it to myself.

I fold my arms over my chest. "Must I really escort you to your room?"

"Can I just have like... five minutes?" he asks, still glancing nervously at the same spot. "I'm getting some fresh air. That's all."

"How about you go to your room *now*, and I *won't* require you to get that extra fresh air by running drills till you drop next week?" I say, cocking a brow. He presses his lips together, and if I didn't know why he was being so squirrely, I'd be seriously concerned. "Schroeder?"

"Fine, I'll go. I'm just gonna..." He sets the stuff he was

holding on the bench next to him, and lucky for the girls, I'm not gonna question it. "Goodnight."

"Night," I say as he hustles inside.

Two flashes of bare skin come around the corner, and I avert my eyes.

"Girls!" I shout in an authoritative tone, and they stop dead.

"Shit," Andi's friend Stella mutters.

"Cover yourselves, and then we'll have a talk about public indecency," I say, gesturing towards items on the bench, trying to maintain a serious face. There's a bit of shuffling, and Andi clears her throat.

"All safe to look, Coach," Andi says in a condescending tone, and I look up to see them both covered in hotel bathrobes. "What are you doing out here?"

"What am *I* doing out here?" I ask, glancing between them. Andi's face is full of amusement, and Stella looks like she's about to shit herself.

"Yeah," Andi presses. "What are *you* doing out here?"

"Girl, shut up," Stella whisper-shouts. "Sorry," she says, turning her attention to me. "You'll have to excuse her. She hasn't learned the proper methods of ass kissing your way out of a problem." I glance at Andi, fighting a laugh. *She knows how to kiss ass just fine.*

"It's past curfew," I say firmly. "And I assume I don't need to remind you nudity is against school rules."

"Of course not," Stella says, clearly panicking. *Poor girl.* "Are you gonna report us?"

"I'm not going to relay this to Dean Riley," I say, and she lets out a breath of relief. "I'll chalk it up to stress from today's events paired with New Year's celebrations. But this is your first and last warning."

"Yes." Stella nods her head profusely. "Thank you. And it'll never happen again, and we're so sorry if you felt violated or anything. And I swear it was a one-time thing. We were completing a stupid bet, and like I said, it'll never ever happen again."

"Yeah," Andi says, rolling her lips together to fight a smile. "We're *soooo* sorry, Coach. We promise you'll never have to see us naked again." *She's asking to be punished.*

"Andi," Stella chastises again. "Stop. Talking."

"Yeah, Ms. Lyons," I say sternly. "The more you open your mouth, the worse the punishment will be."

Stella's eyes widen. "No punishment needed, Coach Porter. Truly."

My eyes swing to Andi's. "Let's go," I instruct. "I'm escorting you back to your rooms."

"Oh, come on," Andi argues. "That's hardly necessary."

I spin around and cock a brow at her. She rolls her eyes, but I can tell by the way she bites her lower lip she's loving this. We return to the hotel lobby and make our way to the elevator. The girls are whispering to each other, and I pretend I don't notice. A bell dings, signaling the elevator's arrival, and I gesture for them to go inside.

"What are your room numbers?" I ask.

"324," Stella replies.

"And yours, Ms. Lyons?" I ask after Andi doesn't reply.

"383," she grumbles. *Well, that's convenient.*

I press the button for the third floor, and silence blankets the elevator as the doors click shut and we begin our ascent.

The tension is thick, and I find myself wishing Andi and I were alone. *Then again, I'd probably have her pinned against the side of the elevator before we reached the second floor.* The bell dings, and the metal doors slide open, yanking me out of the daydream. The girls stroll out, and I follow behind them.

"The escort really isn't necessary," Stella says. "I promise we're heading back to our rooms. Right, Andi?"

"Yeah, totally," Andi says sarcastically.

"I think I'd rather make sure for myself." I smile tightly.

We arrive at Stella's room, and she unlocks the door. She glances between us, mouths *sorry* at Andi, and scurries inside.

The moment the door shuts, Andi turns to me, an annoyed but amused expression on her face.

"Really?" she says. "Was that necessary?"

"You did break the rules."

Andi's smile breaks free as we turn to walk slowly down the dimly lit hallway. "You know," she says quietly, "I *am* naked under this robe."

My eyes slide to hers, jaw ticking. "Don't taunt me, Cupcake."

"I'm not," she replies, putting her hands up in defense. "Just stating facts."

"Oh, really?"

"Yep."

We pause in front of room 365. *My room.* I glance at the handle, the key burning a hole in my pocket. *How easy it would be to go inside and have my way with her.*

"You should go to your room," I choke out.

"I don't know," Andi says, reaching up to push apart the neckline of her robe. I look away, taking in the sight of the totally empty hallway. "God," she says, breathing out. "Have you noticed it's just *soooo* hot in here?"

She attempts to open the tie, and I press my hand against the fabric, pushing her against the door. I drop my forehead to hers, lips inches away. "You're not making this easy."

"I told you I wouldn't."

The ding of the elevator echoes down the hallway, and I swipe my keycard and push us both inside before anyone can see. I spin her around, slamming the door with her back against it. Our eyes connect, heavy breaths filling the room as we both refuse to look away. It was easier to resist this pull to her in the hallway. Now that we're in my empty suite? All bets are off.

I lean down to her ear. "Happy New Year's, Cupcake."

She straightens her shoulders and nudges me off her, causing me to take a step back. She maintains eye contact while bringing a hand to the belt of her robe and unties it. Within seconds, she's gloriously naked in the middle of my hotel room.

"It's been a long week," she says, licking her lips. "And school hasn't actually started yet. So how about we stop denying ourselves and get this out of our systems one more time?"

I step forward, sliding my hand behind her head, and bring her mouth towards mine.

"Just one more time?" I ask, knowing how easy one can turn into ten. *I'm betting on it, in fact.*

"Only once," she repeats.

I stare down at her lips, every breath drawing me closer. Her warm skin in my hands is so familiar, so beautiful. I may be strong, but I'm still a man, and how can I deny this drop dead gorgeous, *horny* woman the simple pleasure of an orgasm? I grip her hips and hoist her onto me, her long legs wrapping around my waist.

"Fuck it."

To be continued...

Want more of Andi and Porter (and Knox)?
Their full length novel will be coming in 2024!

Acknowledgments

As always, the amount of people to thank only grows as my writing journey continues.

I'd first like to thank my husband for supporting our family and allowing me to chase my dreams. I love you exponentially and quite literally couldn't do this without your encouragement.

Thank you to my parents for supporting me in my journey as a writer and never making me feel ashamed for writing about hot people making merry mischief.

Thank you to Alli Morgan, who's my number one girl during this process. When you and I work together... magic. I love you and your beautiful mind.

A very special thank you to Meg Jones, author of ***Invisible String*** and ***Clean,*** for the brilliant idea of the "Dicktionary," and also for letting me steal and reinvent her childhood trauma of sobbing after receiving the wrong color rocking horse.

Thank you to Carolyn Holland, who is an absolute rockstar. You are always eager to help and go above and beyond as a beta. I'm so appreciative of you. Keep writing. I can't wait for your own stories to be out into the world.

Thank you to my beta and sensitivity readers, who have assisted in improving this novel to the very version you have in your hands today. Without you, this book simply would not be the same. Thank you Grace E., Jenn M., Niharika K.,

Katy M., Kayla M., Maria R., Erin M., Mollie G., Kristen H., Ellie G., Ellen M., Bethie H., Emma S., and Caitlin L.

Thank you to my bookish and author friends. Because of you all, I have the motivation to keep going every day: Dany, Addie, Jenn, Mikaela, Sarah, Chiara, Maeve, Isabel, and Gracie. I'm so grateful for our friendships.

Thank you to my incredible editor.

Thank you to my graphic designer, Sandra at Maldo Designs, for creating a beautiful cover and always having the most patience with me.

Thank you to Jessie at Book Blurb Magic for the amazing blurb!

Lastly, I would like to thank you, the reader, for taking a chance and reading Porter and Andi's story. I hope you enjoyed it!

Dick-tionary

Whether you wish to be naughty or nice, while limited in number, it's high in spice. Here's a dick-tionary for you to find, or avoid, the smut that's inside.

- Fifteen
- Sixteen
- Twenty

Spread those pages.

Content Warnings

Please be aware, *Merry Mischief List* contains topics that could be uncomfortable for some readers. These include, but are not limited to, alcohol consumption, vulgar language, mention of a car accident, age gap (10 years), consensual sexually explicit content, light bondage, a MFM (Male/Female/Male) sexual scene, a happy for now ending, and the overt sexualization of Santa Claus and his elves.

Also by Hailey Dickert

Return Policy is the first novel in the Crystal Bay University series by Hailey Dickert. It can be read as a standalone; however, since Sophia is a side character from Dickert's first novel *The Sister Between Us*, it is suggested to read that first for the best experience.

Elijah Anderson

I was the big man on campus.

Everything in my life was going exactly according to plan until a wrecking ball reminded me that there were more important things than touchdowns, booze, and pretty girls.

In the most turbulent time of my life, I felt lost and defeated until the moment my eyes landed on *her*.

Sophia Summers is everything I never knew I wanted. A sweet shot of sunshine in the unrelenting hurricane.

There's just one little problem. She doesn't trust in love, and she definitely doesn't trust me.

But I'm a patient man, and she's worth waiting for. Soon she'll realize that I want every part of her—the darkness, the light, and the shadows in between. I'm already hers, whether she likes it or not.

No returns, no refunds.

Read now on Amazon!

The Sister Between Us is Dickert's debut novel that started it all. This second-chance sports romance tells the story of Jake and Leah.

One night is all it takes to change everything.

Leah Stone

He was my best friend's brother. My neighbor. The one person I was never supposed to fall for, until lines got blurred—stolen kisses and lies told to the people we loved most.

Jake Summers

When the secrets we'd been keeping came out, broken hearts weren't the only casualties. Though I've spent years chasing my dreams of being a professional soccer player, I've never forgotten the one who got away.

A chance encounter brings me back face to face with the only person I've ever loved.

Can we repair what's been broken?

Has time healed the scars that run deeper than the surface?

Will the sister between us bring us back together or push us apart yet again?

Read now on Amazon!

Keep reading for a sneak peek of

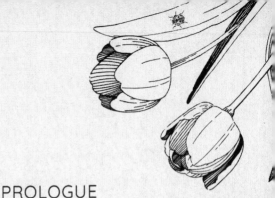

PROLOGUE
SOPHIA

Nine Years Old

"I'm sorry, Sophie Bear. I know you were looking forward to sitting outside," Dad says as I glare at the rain pouring down in sheets.

"You can't control the weather, Papa Bear." I stab the plastic spoon into my ice cream. "It's fine."

It is not fine.

"Well, *anyways*," Sage, my best friend, mumbles with a mouth full of rocky road, "tell your dad about that epic drawing you did of the soccer player for Friday's fall showcase!"

"Oh, is that this week?" Dad asks.

Mom would have remembered.

"Yup," I tell my bowl, mind wandering to *my* favorite picture of a little clay teapot. A few months ago, Chloe, my sister, and her best friend, Leah, were making one in our garage while laughing and singing. Hopefully one day I'll be able to draw their smiling faces too, but for now, that's what I can do. The sketch reminds me of home—*the feeling, not the place.*

My twin siblings are nine years older than me, but they never fail to make me feel included and loved. Especially my older brother, Jake. He thinks we don't notice all the small stuff he does since Mom's been gone, but I do. I notice every single thing down to the burnt pancakes. *They taste better that way anyway.*

"I can't wait." Dad beams, eating a big bite of his chocolate sundae. A loud ring blares throughout the small shop. He sticks his spoon in the bowl before pulling his phone from his pocket and sliding out of the booth.

"How's the mint chocolate chip, Joey?" Sage asks, using the nickname she gave me because of my obsession with koalas. *You make one horrible Australian zookeeper impersonation and never live it down.*

"Everything I dreamed and more." I grin, fighting off her spoon as she tries to steal some.

Dad clears his throat, interrupting our battle for the bite. "We gotta go, girls." He chucks his half-eaten sundae in the trash. "Come on."

"Why?" I ask, eyes glued to the sugary goodness he just wasted. "Can we bring our ice cream?"

"I don't care, let's go." His strange tone has Sage and I sliding quickly out of the booth.

The drive is so quiet I'm afraid to ask where we're going. My ice cream is turning into soup, and I try to focus on the rain pitter-pattering against the truck to calm my nerves. A flash of lightning followed by a rumbling thunder rattles me to my bones, stealing my sense of security. *I hate thunder-*

storms. I'm surprised Dad even drove in this weather. He always gets on Jake and Chloe about being careful when it's raining outside.

We turn into a large parking lot, passing a bright sign that reads Longwood Hospital.

"Dad?" I ask, my voice trembling as he parks the truck. "Why are we here? What's going on?"

"Come on, girls," he says, ignoring my questions and hopping out. *Why is he ignoring me?* We follow him through the torrential downpour to the emergency room, ice cream bowls in hand. Dad instructs us to sit in the farthest corner of the room with the promise he'll be right back.

The air conditioning hits my damp skin, sending shivers through my body. My shaking fingers stick to the soggy paper bowl, and I consider looking for a trash can and a bathroom to clean up. *But what if I miss something? Dad said to stay right here.* My eyes fall to the little plastic spoon clinking to the floor.

"I'll throw it away," Sage offers quietly, taking the bowl.

"Thanks."

A wave of nausea hits me at the scent of the room. *It's too clean.* I stare at a hole in the mint-green wall. It's about the size of a fist.

What made someone so mad?

My dad's pleading voice snaps my attention to him. "Please," he begs the doctor. "Please tell me they're going to be okay."

My shoulders shake, and a loud bang has me jump in my seat. Jake runs through the emergency room doors like a soaking wet bat out of hell. His panicked face makes my heart beat faster than it ever has before.

Jake is okay.

Knowing my brother is alive and well calms my anxiety momentarily until I hear the words "Chloe," "Leah," and "accident." Then my stomach drops back to my feet.

Sage must have returned at some point because her arms are tight around me as tears blur my vision. "They're going to be fine, Joey," she whispers.

I struggle to calm my rapid breathing as Jake talks with the doctors. His face is scrunched tight like he's in pain.

What's going on?

Two of my favorite people in the world are just behind those doors, and no one will tell me anything. Dad always thinks I'm too young to join the "grown-up conversations," but I'm almost *ten*. I deserve to know what's going on with my family.

I'm not as oblivious as everyone thinks I am.

I can handle the truth.

The door Jake just slammed through opens again, and Autumn, Sage's mom, comes into the waiting room. My mom should be the one coming through those doors, but here I am, in a hospital on the scariest day of my life, with her nowhere to be seen. *What could be more important than this?*

I roll my eyes, turning my attention to my stuck together fingers, and slowly pull them apart.

Autumn bends down in front of us with open arms. "Hey, girls." I tilt my head. *What in the world is going on?*

She pulls us both in for a tight hug, and I glance up to the sight of Jake collapsing against Dad's chest as his sobs echo off every wall in the room. His pained cry pierces me like the devil's claws, digging in, dragging me down to a nightmare I never expected to be mine.

CHAPTER 1
SOPHIA

Eighteen Years Old

"You know what you're missing?" Sage asks, halting in place on the pathway toward the springs. She grabs my shoulder, spinning me around to unzip my backpack, and Charlie shrugs with an amused grin.

Question: how much bullshit are you willing to endure just to make your friends happy?

Answer: the limit does not exist.

Sage rezips my bag and turns me back around, bringing two empty hands over my head.

"What in the ever-loving hell are you doing?" I ask.

"Putting on your party girl hat." She smiles sweetly. "You've clearly forgotten it was in there."

My shoulders sag as I blow out a heavy breath. "I'm sorry." To avoid ruining the night for everyone, I play along, bringing my hands above my head and repositioning the invisible hat. "My party girl hat is now properly in place." *So is the burning pit in my stomach.*

"That's our girl," Sage says, throwing an arm over my shoulder. "I didn't siphon the good shit from my parents' liquor cabinet all year, risking eternal grounding, to *not* get shit-faced with my girls on the night of our high school graduation."

"Come on," Charlie chimes in, adding her arm over Sage's. My shoulders are heavy, but I savor the familiar weight of my two best friends holding me close. "Only a few more months till we're at Crystal Bay University, living it up as college freshmen." She cocks a dark brow. "That's something to celebrate."

Change rarely comes easily to me, but moving to CBU is one transition I'm definitely ready for. Maybe I'll finally find some distraction from the swarming thoughts plaguing me at every turn of these familiar back roads.

We arrive at the crowded springs full of fellow high school graduates. The sun dances behind the trees, and although it's cooler than the sweltering graduation earlier, it's a typical late summer afternoon in Florida.

The sunshine state—aka the only place on Earth that's hotter and wetter than the devil's asshole.

We find our way to the drinks table, and Sage adds half a bottle of vodka. Charlie brought four wine coolers, and I set my pathetic contribution of orange juice for mixers on the table. Tucked away in my backpack is a flask of top shelf whiskey I "borrowed" from Dad... but I'm saving that for myself.

It doesn't seem to matter though. There's enough alcohol

here to last a month. I'm not sure how a bunch of minors got full bottles of liquor, but *cheers, bitch.*

I spot a handle of Jack Daniels on the table and pour myself a whiskey and ginger ale as Sage and Charlie fill their tumblers with vodka and orange juice.

The girls and I amble along the water's edge, where people are laughing and splashing in the golden sunlight. We set down our things near where the entirety of last year's Longwood High football team is playing beer pong.

My eyes drift around the springs, snagging on *him.* The face of my nightmares—the bane of my existence—my ex-boyfriend Seth Miller. And what is the piece of shit doing? Laughing like he's the happiest person in the world. Like he's just a guy partying with his friends on graduation night. Like the moment permanently imprinted in my mind every time I close my eyes never happened.

How can he act like nothing happened?

Seth drags a hand through his blonde hair, turning around. His eyes connect with mine, and repressed memories surge to the surface. His lips curl upward, and yep, I'm definitely going to be sick.

"Hey," Sage says, snapping my attention back to her sympathetic eyes. "Stop worrying about him. He's not worth your time." Sage doesn't know the true reason for our breakup, but she's my best friend, and if I hate someone, so does she. No questions asked.

"You're right." I lock away my hatred for him so she won't get suspicious of just how deep it runs.

"Of course I am," Sage says.

Charlie's boyfriend, Jonathan, waves to her, blowing a kiss, and she blushes, sipping her drink. They've been dating since freshman year and will no doubt get married and have babies before the rest of us have even finished college. They were the "it" couple at our school—head cheerleader and varsity football quarterback. Totally cliche and totally adorable.

I wrinkle my nose at her. "You guys are so cute."

She grins sheepishly. "Thanks."

"How do you feel about next year?" I ask her timidly, knowing it's a touchy subject.

Charlie lets out a heavy exhale. "I mean, we're going to schools on opposite sides of the state." She looks down at the liquid in her cup before taking a big gulp, doing a little shimmy as it goes down. "So not looking forward to the distance."

"Jonathan will have Seth," Sage says, and I tense at his name. "They can stroke each other's dicks."

I chuckle and shake my head, trying to dispel the visual image. "And you'll have us to keep you plenty busy."

"That *is* true," Charlie says, tipping her glass towards us.

Jonathan walks up, sliding an arm around Charlie's waist and pulling her to him. "Hey, beautiful."

"Hey, babe." Charlie beams, nuzzling into his chest.

"Ladies." He gestures to us with his cup in a cheers motion.

"Jonathan," we coo back.

"Wanna go for a walk?" Jonathan asks Charlie, and she looks to us as if for permission.

"Go." I wave her off.

"Yeah," Sage says, slapping Charlie on the ass. "Get outta here."

"Okay, okay." Charlie laughs, protecting her butt with one hand as she turns away and joins Jonathan.

"Hey, beautiful girls," our friend Benji says, throwing an arm around Sage's shoulders.

"Benji." She smirks up at him. He's a horrible flirt and their relationship is purely platonic, but they both know how to have a good time.

"I've got some party favors if you're interested?" He presents a Ziploc with a few joints.

She turns her eyes back to mine, the wheels in her brain spinning on overdrive.

"Sage." I let out a soft chuckle. "I'm not a wounded dog. I can keep myself busy. Go have fun."

"You wanna come?" Benji asks, dangling the little baggie between his fingers. "I've got plenty."

"I'm good. Think I'll go play a round of pong." I gesture over my shoulder toward the beer pong tournament I have no intention of joining. "You guys have fun."

"Okay, we'll come find you in a bit." Sage squeezes my shoulder, and then they're gone.

The golden hour from the sun is still emitting plenty of light, so I down the rest of my drink, toss the cup in a trash can, and head towards the woods. I glance around, making sure Seth is distracted and doesn't see me leave. I have no interest in talking to him tonight. Especially alone.

He's enthralled in a conversation with one of the other guys on the football team. I make my escape, venturing down the path towards a quiet rock, away from the party. Leah, my bonus sister, has brought me here a few times. It's her favorite place to get away and think. I settle on the cool rock, placing my backpack next to me, and unzip it to pull out my notebook and a pencil. The interior pages are blank, without lines, which is perfect for my particular usage.

Spinning the pencil between my fingers, I fight the urge to draw what always slips to the forefront of my mind. The face I've drawn for years but somehow never tire of looking at. I draw her as a child, a teenager, what she'd have looked like if she grew up and had kids. I've drawn it all and somehow, I never run out of ideas. The current one I'm working on is what she would've looked like at high school graduation. It's a closeup of her face wearing a graduation cap flung to the side.

I sigh at my unhealthy obsession and unscrew the flask, then take a swig of the deliciously potent whiskey. The strong liquid glides down my throat, leaving a familiar burn in its wake.

As I put the finishing touches on my drawing, a rustling in the bushes steals my attention, and my heart stops beating. *Please don't be Seth.*

"Who's there?" I shout in attempted bravery. My hands tremble as leaves crunch beneath someone's heavy feet, the sound growing closer by the second. Breathing is a distant memory, and I might pass out if the person doesn't reveal themself soon.

"I come in peace," a male voice says. The unfamiliar husky tone laced with humor relieves my anxieties as a tall figure steps out of the bush, holding his hands up in surrender.

Holy shit. I've died and gone to hot guy heaven.

The spitting image of all my favorite fictional men come to life is standing before me with delicious chocolate brown hair and a panty-soaking, crooked grin. He rubs a hand along his sharp jawline, and adorable dimples pop through as he smirks at me. A tattoo peeks out from his v-neck T-shirt, with more running along his arms. *Am I dreaming?* I dig my fingernails into my palm. *Nope, that definitely hurt.*

"You going to say anything, or are you just gonna keep eye fucking me?" he asks as his gaze rakes over my body, eliciting a shiver.

"I was not *eye fucking* you!" *Liar, liar, panties on fire.* "You caught me by surprise. I thought I was out here alone."

"And I thought my devilish good looks shocked your pretty mouth speechless."

My lips part, and then I smash them shut. "Wow, aren't you *hilarious?*"

"I try." He winks, and I clench my thighs together as his eyes drop to the sketchbook on my lap. *Is it getting hotter out here or is it just me?* "What are you doing sitting here alone instead of at that party?"

"Oh, uh…" I'm definitely not about to tell this stranger the truth. *I'm avoiding my overbearing ex like a coward.* "My friends were momentarily busy, so I thought I'd slip away for a bit of doodling."

"Doodling?"

"Mm-hmm."

"Can I see said doodles?" he asks, taking a few steps closer and extending his hand, presumably for my sketchbook. *Yeah, fat chance.*

"Ha." I fake laugh. "Absolutely not." I snap the sketchbook closed and shove it into my backpack, zipping it shut. If he saw I drew the same face repeatedly, he'd think I was a stalker. Sure, I draw other things too. But most of the time, she's my favorite subject.

When I turn back to face him, his sideways grin has turned into a full toothed smile.

"What?" I ask, unable to keep my lips from curling up.

"Nothin'." He shoves his hands in his pockets. "Just you dramatically hiding the notebook in your bag makes me all the more curious."

"I am *not* dramatic," I scoff, folding my arms across my chest. He raises his dark brows, eyes flicking down at my pushed-up chest before returning to mine.

Oops, I definitely forgot I was wearing a low-cut dress.

"Whatever you say, Sunflower."

I cock my brow. "Sunflower?"

"Yeah, *Sunflower*." He waves a hand at my torso, and my eyes drop to the little pastel sunflowers dancing across my dress.

"Very creative," I tease, attempting to stop the corners of my lips from turning upwards but failing with flying Technicolor.

"I tend to be quite creative, yes."

"What are *you* doing out here? I can't imagine you're from Longwood. I think I'd remember someone who looks like you." The words escape before I can think better of them. If I could slap my forehead without looking like a damn dork, I would.

He raises a curious eyebrow. "Like *me*?"

"Yeah, someone all tall, dark, and brooding." I bite my lower lip to camouflage a smirk.

"What makes you think I'm brooding?"

"You have this… intense thing about you. Like you're all intelligent and mysterious." The smile breaks through at the thought of one of my favorite brooding men. "It's very Stefan Salvatore."

"Stefan Salva-*who*?" He furrows his brows.

"Never mind." I wave him off. "And besides, you're *also* here talking to me instead of enjoying the festivities, so I don't think *you're* the party boy type."

"You seem to know a lot about me," he quips, obviously amused.

I shrug. "I'm good at figuring people out."

"Oh, is that so? And what else have you figured out about me?" His arm veins bulge as he folds them across his chest.

Fuck, he's sexy.

"Hmm." I tap my finger to my lips. "I think you're a little cocky. You deflect using humor. You're nosy." I raise my brows at him. "I think you're completely aware of how good-looking you are."

"You think I'm good-looking?" He grins, waggling his eyebrows.

"Let me finish." I hold up a hand. "You're aware of it, but you don't seem to let it go to your head. Otherwise, you'd probably be shirtless by the water, trying to pick up a cheerleader rather than talking to the girl who's avoiding that party like the plague."

"Wow." He nods while rubbing a hand over his mouth. "You figured all that stuff out after a two-minute conversation? Either you're incredibly perceptive or I'm embarrassingly predictable."

"Let's call it a tie." I smirk, enjoying his playfulness. "What I can't figure out... is what you're doing at this party when you so clearly aren't from around here. No one local would wear pure white Nikes to the dirty ass springs." I gesture to his mud-splattered tennis shoes, and he looks down before returning his amused gaze to mine.

"Oh well." He shrugs. "What are shoes for if not to be worn?"

"More witty banter and questions left unanswered." I roll my eyes teasingly.

"Well, I am *not* from around here. As you suspected, Sherlock." He shifts on his heels. "I'm here visiting family and my... uh, brother told me there would probably be a party here tonight if I wanted to get out of the house. So..."

"Oh, is your brother here tonight too?"

"Nah," he responds, shaking his head. "He's older."

"Is it your first time in Longwood?"

"Yeah, I came to meet my... dad," he says with a pained expression. I want to reach out and smooth the wrinkles caused by the frown.

"To *meet* your dad?" I hardly know this guy, but there's this intense desire to learn everything about him.

"My *biological* dad. He wasn't around growing up." A heavy breath escapes him. "A lot of... shit happened earlier this year. So I took the week off to come meet him."

"Weren't you ever curious who he was?"

He looks down at his hands, wringing them together. "I mean... not really. But I made a promise to give Mark a chance so... here I am."

My brows raise upward. "Wow, that must be a lot for you to deal with."

"Yeah," he says sheepishly. "It has been... Sorry, my head's just a jumbled mess, so I guess you're the victim of my inevitable brain dump."

"No apologies needed." My head shakes as I smile reassuringly. "I'm a good listener."

"Yeah?"

"Yep. Certified problem solver," I say, waving a hand at my body.

"Well, how about you tell me why you're out here doodling instead of hanging out with your friends or... *boyfriend?*" He says the last part like a question, and the knife twists painfully in my chest.

"No boyfriend here, single as a Pringle," I mumble. Chloe and Leah said that phrase so many times, but it sounds lame as fuck coming out of my mouth. "And, uh, I'm avoiding someone," I admit.

"Interesting." He narrows his eyes and takes a few long strides toward me. "May I?" he asks, gesturing toward the rock, and I scoot over, allowing him to sit next to me. His shoulder is centimeters away from mine, radiating enough heat to melt titanium. I breathe in through my nose, and the intoxicating scent of his cologne floods my senses, wreaking havoc on my insides.

"Are you wearing Versace?" I ask to fill the silence.

"Were you watching through my bathroom window as I got ready tonight?"

"No... I just happen to like that scent." I don't admit to smelling the men's cologne samples at the mall and assigning them to my favorite book boyfriends. In case anyone is wondering, Nathan Hawkins smells like Giorgio Armani Acqua di Giò.

"Good to know..." He smirks, looking out at the stream. "You come here often?"

A laugh bubbles out of me. *"That's* the best line you could come up with?"

"I'm not hittin' on you," he says cooly, and I fight the disappointment begging to appear on my face. *Why the hell would I be disappointed?* "I meant do you come to this rock a lot, or did you just discover this little hideaway?"

"I come here when I need to clear my head... or escape reality for a bit."

"And is it clear now?"

"Well, this annoying stranger kind of interrupted my self-reflection, so I'll have to get back to you on that." A snarky smile spreads across my face.

"Ha ha." He wrinkles his nose at me, and I struggle not to blush at how cute he looks. "Well, I *have* been told I'm an excellent listener as well, so... you know... if you wanna talk about it?"

He shifts position, and his shoulder bumps mine. Given how he looks, I assumed if he touched me, I'd spontaneously combust or be struck by a bolt of lightning, but the only thing happening is my heart rate accelerating faster than a hummingbird's wings.

"Trust me, you don't want to go down that rabbit hole," I reply. "It's taken my therapist years to unpack the baggage that is Sophia's life."

"How about the condensed version?" he asks, without even a hint of judgment in his voice.

"I'm going to scare you right off this rock," I say, connecting my gaze with his.

"Is that something you'd care about?"

"What?"

"If I left," he asks with a straight face, although there's a slight upward curve of his plump lips.

"Maybe," I say honestly. Although I can't pinpoint why. I don't get attached to people anymore. In fact, I usually push people away so hard they go running for the hills. I especially don't confide in total strangers. My therapist says it's because I have abandonment issues. But what does she know?

"Well, I promise to not go running for the hills," he says as if reading my damn mind. *Who the hell is this guy?* "If you promise you're not a serial killer."

"I am *not* a serial killer."

"I figured." His eyes drop to my feet, then venture slowly back to my face, and damn if it doesn't set me on fire. "What are the chances of there being two of us out here?"

The fire's doused momentarily before I realize he's kidding, of course, and I hit him playfully on the arm. "Hey, don't ruin this spot for me with your Ted Bundy talk."

"Sorry, sorry." He laughs, throwing his hands up, expression softening. "So what's clouding that pretty little head of yours, Sunflower?"

Read 'Return Policy' to continue Sophia and Elijah's story!

About the Author

Hailey (Bruhn) Dickert is a contemporary romance author born in a small coastal Florida town who grew up writing songs in her bedroom. She previously maintained a personal blog documenting her journey of moving abroad to her adopted hometown in Germany.

Dickert's debut novel, *The Sister Between Us*, was released April 2023, immediately hitting the Amazon Top 100. *Return Policy*, her second novel, was released June 2023, also immediately hitting the Amazon Top 100.

When she's not writing at her kitchen table or in her favorite local brewery, Sailfish Brewing Company, Dickert spends most of her time reading, making memories with her husband and young son, and traveling. An admitted sports fanatic, she feeds her addiction to football by watching the Miami Dolphins and Minnesota Vikings games on Sunday afternoons.

Keep in touch with Hailey Dickert via the web:
Website: haileydickert.com
Facebook: @haileydickert
Instagram: @haileydickertauthor
TikTok: @haileydickertauthor

Printed in Great Britain
by Amazon

35737005R00117